SECRETS AND LIES

SHAY LACY

author of *Touchpoint* and *Counterpoint*

CRIMSON ROMANCE

F+W Media, Inc.

This edition published by
Crimson Romance
an imprint of F+W Media, Inc.
10151 Carver Road, Suite 200
Blue Ash, Ohio 45242
www.crimsonromance.com

ISBN 10: 1-4405-6711-5
ISBN 13: 978-1-4405-6711-7
eISBN 10: 1-4405-6712-3
eISBN 13: 978-1-4405-6712-4

Dedication

Life offers us chances to make a difference. You can be the change that you want to see in the world. My thanks to all the people who use their chances and make this world a better place.

Thanks to Crimson Romance for believing in my work. To Maumee Valley RWA, whose members uplift each other, cheer for achievements, and offer hugs during times of struggle. To the B-I-C group for online accountability and support, and to my fellow Panera Prison inmates who leave the house to write. Special thanks to Ray Wenck, Constance Phillips, and Jenna Rutland, whose friendship has been invaluable. And, as always, my thanks to my husband, who encourages me to do what I love.

CHAPTER 1

Why would somebody steal a sculpture of a fertility god instead of buying Viagra? Private investigator Charlie Ziffkin had followed the thief's trail from Hollywood to Miami, proving this was no petty thief. His actions suggested he worked for a client—a rich one. Charlie needed to find out who had that kind of money for illegal activities. Who better to help him locate his client's fertility statue than a hooker? He hoped to get lucky on this street where they stood on every corner. He'd start with prostitutes and work his way up the food chain.

He smiled at the brunette in the barely-there mini as he approached.

The hooker's eyes glinted in the streetlight as her gaze ran over him from head to toe. "Hey, baby, I can make you feel real good." Up close, even the night and her heavy makeup couldn't conceal the wear and tear her lifestyle had caused.

"I'd like to feel good." Wasn't that the truth. Since his brother, Billy's, senseless murder two years ago, he hadn't felt anything but pain. "But what I need is information." So he could retrieve his client's property and get out of this town where he'd been born. Where Billy was buried. Why the hell had the thief come here, of all places?

The hooker's mascara-heavy lashes had been at half-mast as she'd leaned toward him. Now her eyes opened fully and filled with wariness. She took a step back. "I don't talk to cops."

"I'm not a cop. My name is Chaz. I'm out here from Hollywood for a few days looking to get connected, you know what I mean? I have lots of friends back home. I need a way to make them happy. You must know who to talk to when you want to have a large party. I'm sure you know all kinds of things, like who holds the money and power in this town. If I wanted something and I didn't want people asking a lot of questions, who would I talk to?"

"What do you do in Hollywood?"

"I'm a promoter."

Her suspicious gaze raked him. "You're mighty young."

"Age is meaningless if you can get things done. And I can."

"Baby, listen, if you're not interested in the merchandise, I need to make a living." She glanced around as though looking for another john.

"How much?"

Her sly gaze swung to his face. She ran her tongue slowly over her upper lip. "For you, good looking, thirty bucks."

Charlie pulled his wallet out of his suit jacket pocket and retrieved the money. He'd better not have to pay everybody for information on this job. His client had offered a hefty fee, but he'd only gotten a retainer upfront. He held the bills out toward her. As she reached for them with long purple fingernails, he said, "I need names."

"See Carlos at the Bottoms Up bar on Hialeah. He's there every night. He'll know who can help you." She snatched the money and stuffed it into her neon blue bra. A sultry smile lifted the corners of her red lips. "I can get rid of that tension you feel."

He was losing his acting ability if she could see that. He forced his muscles to relax and gave her a slow smile. "You've helped me already. Thanks. If you're ever in Hollywood … "

She shrugged. "Sure, baby." She strutted away on sparkling stilettos.

A blonde hooker lounged under the streetlight at the next corner. He fought the urge to jog toward her because he needed answers *now*. He couldn't linger in Miami. His parents and brother, Michael, whom he hadn't seen since Billy's funeral, lived here. He couldn't face them knowing he lived while Billy's body lie in a grave just miles from here. *Too close*.

Billy had been brilliant, with a PhD and a new job as a research scientist. He probably would have cured cancer if he'd lived. But a freak robbery turned murder had buried those dreams. The police thought it might have been somebody high on drugs or looking for money for their next fix. His murderer had never been caught.

Charlie, on the other hand, had been a mediocre student who'd only cared about one thing—acting. He'd lit out of Miami for Hollywood thinking he only had to arrive to fulfill his dreams. A dozen years later, success still eluded him. In professional terms, he was a failure.

But he was trying to right the wrong of living. He couldn't be Billy, couldn't take over where his brother's life had ended. But Charlie could succeed instead of fail. He could make life better for others, one case at a time. This was the biggest case he'd worked so far. Retrieving Hollywood producer Jordan Hessler's stolen relic would guarantee him referrals and success. He just had to find it and escape Miami before his past sucked him back in.

In the next block, a young Latina spoke to a john. She reminded him of his childhood and teenage sweetheart, Juliana Sanchez. She'd been his greatest supporter, participating in every dramatic endeavor he dreamed up. Rarely did a day pass when she wasn't playing pirates or detectives or space aliens with him and, as they got older, Romeo and Juliet. It had been just acting, until one day it wasn't acting anymore. Charlie didn't know when he'd fallen in love with her, somewhere around age fifteen. They'd had two years together where he'd had to hide how he felt from his best friend, afraid his heart would burst at the mere sight of her.

Then Juliana's mother died, and her father had sent her to live with her aunt until he could sell their house. Sergeant Sanchez had severed all contact between Juliana and Charlie. He should have taken his police revolver and killed Charlie; that would have been kinder. Thirteen years apart and, still, no woman had ever measured up to Juliana. He didn't think one ever would.

As far as he knew, she still lived here. For years after she'd been ripped from his arms and his life he'd wanted—needed—to run into her. But he couldn't see her like this. He was the walking dead. She deserved better than him.

Charlie drew on his acting skills. He forced his face to relax into a smile as he approached the blonde. He had to make the hooker feel safe so she'd provide the intel he needed.

• • •

"This bra is killing me," Juliana Sanchez muttered toward the microphone hidden in her long brown hair. In her opinion, push-up bras could be used as instruments of torture.

"It looks *fine* from here, sugar," Vice Detective Hector Muñoz drawled into her earpiece. "So fine."

She smiled toward where her protection watched from a white panel van down the street.

"Better hope her daddy doesn't catch her wearing that outfit," his partner, Detective Karl Polaris, retorted. "He's smart enough to put two and two together, and then he'll do worse than break us back to beat cops. I can't believe I let you talk me into this."

Juliana should be worried, too. If her dad, Police Captain Alejandro Sanchez, found out she was subbing for her friend in vice, he'd break her back to… Gee, what was worse than treating her like a teenager instead of a woman nearly thirty? She was stifling under his overprotectiveness. His behavior had been understandable after her mother was killed and Juliana was injured when a drunk driver had hit their car, but that was over a decade ago. Since then, he'd remarried and had two young sons who enjoyed more freedom than she did. They'd probably even get to be cops when they grew up, unlike her, who did medical transcription for a living. Damn it, she was an adult living on her own. When was he going to think of her as one?

She couldn't regret this act of defiance; after all, she was helping the police like he'd taught her to do. It wasn't her fault her dreams of being a police officer had gone up in smoke in that same accident when a head injury had awoken a psychic talent, making her unfit for police work. If only she'd ignored the strange tingling sensation that began at her fingertips and helped her "find" lost items—her father's keys, her aunt's missing shoe, her school friend who'd been abducted by an estranged parent—or learn things about an object when she held something connected to it. If she'd kept it to herself, she never would have learned she had the gift of psychometry.

It was too late now to keep her psychic gift secret. She helped the police where she could, normally the burglary department, with her father's blessing. But sometimes she had to sneak to do it. She lifted her chin and pulled her shoulders back, a mistake wearing this bra. Her nipples nearly popped out. Damn. And this barely-there skirt let the unseasonably cool Miami night air blow right up her crotch. Talk about a cold shower.

She tried to strut like the rest of the streetwalkers on this downtown strip of neon sidewalk. The five-inch silver stiletto heels were killing her, too. No wonder prostitutes were so eager to get flat on their backs.

Muffling a laugh, she gave a come-hither smile to a middle-aged balding man in a lightweight suit as he approached. He looked over her goods and kept on walking.

"Not in the mood, I guess," she said.

"Keep walking," Hector instructed. "There's some more prospects up ahead."

A dark-haired man was talking to a bleached blonde in a purple sequined mini-dress just a little ahead. The blonde looked eager—her feet probably hurt. The man was a smooth operator; Juliana could tell by the way he leaned toward her and ran a finger down her outer arm.

The blonde looked confused, then outraged, and then she smiled once more, sucked in by whatever the man said to soothe her. Maybe he was kinky but the blonde was willing for a price. Juliana got close enough to hear his smooth baritone and cajoling tone.

"My name is Chaz. I know people in the industry."

Juliana's steps faltered and she nearly fell over. *No! That name with that voice and that dark wavy hair—it couldn't be!*

But he turned his head, and his profile was as she remembered, except for the two-day stubble that hid his stubborn chin and slight dimple. He'd been seventeen and skinny when her father had sent her to live with her aunt. Now he was a man. And what a man. He'd filled out through the chest and shoulders. He looked sexy. Her heart pounded so hard at seeing him she could hardly think.

For most of her childhood she'd seen him daily. They'd acted out scenes from every play and movie he knew. She'd been Bonnie to his Clyde, Princess Leia to his Han Solo, Tonto to his Lone Ranger. He'd created worlds out of pure imagination, and taken her there with him. Anything had been possible by his side. She could be anything or anyone, and so could he.

And now he was picking up a hooker?

The thought startled her so badly his name leapt from her throat. "Charlie Ziffkin, what are you doing?"

Charlie whirled, and his summer blue gaze flew to her face. He looked like he'd been goosed. "Juliana?"

"Juliana!" echoed in her earpiece. "What are you doing?" Hector sounded like he was coming unhinged.

The blonde latched onto Charlie's arm. "Get lost, ho. He's taken." Her long nails were blood red against his dark sleeve.

"Keep your mind on business!" Hector demanded.

"Now, ladies," Charlie soothed as he slipped his arm from the blonde's grasp. "There's no need for name-calling. Trixie, I'm so sorry. Perhaps another time?" He always was a sweet talker.

Trixie gave Juliana a withering look and minced away on her five-inch spiked heels, working her scantily clad booty for all it was worth.

Then Juliana and Charlie were alone for the first time in thirteen years. Unexpected excitement pulsed through her body at his nearness. Her breaths shortened, and her heart raced. Tension pooled in her lower belly. She'd lusted after the skinny boy, but that paled compared to how the fully grown man made her feel. Now she knew what it felt like to make love. What might it be like to consummate what they'd started so long ago?

"Juliana, make a move," Karl prompted.

Charlie was getting an eyeful of her cleavage and everything else her outfit exposed. At last he looked her in the eyes again with dilated pupils. "You've grown up."

"So have you." She forced herself to take a step toward him, then another, until she could touch him. His heat rolled over her, making her sweat. Her pulse punched into overdrive. Her mouth dried. He would have been her first if her father hadn't stopped them.

She walked her fingers up the sleeve of his black suit jacket. He wore it with a high-collared maroon vest underneath, the collar standing up around his neck, and a black t-shirt under that. With stonewashed jeans, he looked trendy and sexy.

She licked her lips. "You look mighty fine, Charlie."

"I like what I see, too." His finger skimmed her bare arm, giving her goose bumps.

"Want to finish what we started all those years ago?"

His face lowered toward hers. His breath stirred the hair beside her face. He smelled like mint. "Do you need money, Juliana?"

"Everybody needs money." She gave him a steamy look. It wasn't hard.

"How much?"

"For fifty bucks I could ease that itch in your pants." She nodded to the sizable bulge in his jeans.

"Your father wouldn't stop us this time?"

Juliana winced inwardly. Her father wouldn't, but his minions would. "No," she purred. "We could go all the way."

Charlie stared at her with an intensity she couldn't define. She wished they were having this conversation under different circumstances. She dared not take too deep a breath for fear her heart would crack.

From inside his suit jacket he pulled out a black wallet. Juliana's smile felt ready to fracture. He handed the bills to her. It was like pushing through thick mud to reach him.

Their fingers touched. Despite him being a john, a thrill ran through her. She thought she saw sadness in his eyes, which made no sense. The moment seemed frozen. There was only Charlie and the shattering of a young girl's dream. He'd been her hero, even when he'd played the villain.

"Freeze, sleazebag!" Hector yelled, pointing his automatic at Charlie. She hadn't even heard him approach.

Karl materialized from behind Charlie, gun drawn. "Hands on the back of your head and lace your fingers together."

"Step away from him, Juliana," Hector ordered.

"Ah." A smile tugged at one side of Charlie's mouth, sexy and knowing. His blue eyes sparkled like sunlight off a tropical bay. "The family business." He put his hands on his head and interlaced his fingers.

Hector glared at him. "Shut up, scum."

"You're making a mistake." Was that laughter in Charlie's voice?

Karl was rough patting him down. Charlie never took his eyes off Juliana. Why did he think this was funny?

"You're under arrest for solicitation—" Hector began.

"You'd better look in my wallet," Charlie interrupted, even as Karl cuffed him.

Hector's eyebrows lifted. "You offering us a bribe?"

"No, I'm trying to save you some humiliation."

"He was always a good liar," Juliana informed the vice cops.

"Don't believe me then." Charlie shrugged. Hard to do with his hands cuffed behind him.

Hector reached into Charlie's jacket and pulled out his wallet. Flipping it open, he frowned. "You're a private investigator?"

Juliana's mouth fell open, but she recovered enough to say, "He is not. He's a Hollywood actor."

"Retired," Charlie said, smiling.

"It's not true," Juliana insisted.

"I'm on a case."

"You were trying to get laid."

He quirked a dark brow. "Do you think I have to pay women to sleep with me?"

Juliana closed her mouth with a snap. She couldn't imagine any woman saying no to him. "You offered me money for sex."

"I offered you money because I felt sorry for you. I thought something terrible must have happened for you to turn to prostitution. I did it for old time's sake."

Hector waved the wallet. "It doesn't matter what you say. Until this checks out, you're going to the station for booking."

"Ask that prostitute, Trixie, what I wanted from her," Charlie said.

All of them looked in the direction she'd gone, but the street was deserted.

"Guess your witness split," Karl said.

"You're going downtown after all." Hector's smile lit up his swarthy face.

"You want to set up someplace else while Karl runs him in?" Juliana asked. She didn't want to go to the station with Charlie.

"Sure. Let's go over to Second Avenue and see what we can catch."

"See you around, Juliana," Charlie called as Karl led him away. His eyes still sparkled.

Not if I see you first. She climbed into the van with Hector, wishing, for once, that Charlie hadn't been acting and had told the truth.

• • •

"Ziffkin." Hernandez, the portly Latino booking clerk at the police station, stared at Charlie's paperwork. "Any relation to Rick Ziffkin?"

Charlie tried not to react. "Brother." How'd this cop know Rick? Last he'd heard, Rick was a police detective in Fort Lauderdale.

"Then you should know better than to solicit a prostitute."

"I wasn't."

Hernandez held up a meaty hand. "I heard the story. You're still going to cool your heels in here until we check it out."

Charlie sighed. He hadn't foreseen this delay. But then he hadn't expected to meet Juliana Sanchez in hooker clothes. After Hernandez locked him in a cell, he sat down to wait.

Juliana Sanchez. Her name melted like chocolate mint ice cream in his mouth—delectable with impact. A face of sculpted bones and those dark Sophia Loren eyes beckoned men to sin. *Mama mia!* His body still hummed with excitement, and he was still partially aroused. Wavy, dark brown hair fell to her breasts … and what breasts they were. Mounds to dive into and make love to for hours. They were more mouthwatering now than when she'd been sixteen and offered him his heart's desire. His palms itched to touch them. He'd had his hands on her breasts back then, but he'd swear she had more now. Maybe she had implants. No, breasts like hers were real.

Legs a man wanted wrapped around him in the throes of passion. Full pouty lips a man wanted to kiss for hours and then watch surround his cock. God, he ached for her.

She was lovelier and sexier now than she'd been when she'd captured his teenage heart. He'd thought he'd die every time he saw her. One day she was the girl next door, his best friend, the person he told all his dreams to, and the next she was … well, more.

Watching her walk home from the bus stop in her Catholic school uniform had given him a daily hard-on. He'd wanted to lift that plaid skirt and plunge his dick into her.

And then one day out of the blue she'd offered herself to him. He couldn't get her on her back fast enough. He'd gotten his hands inside her blouse, her panties off and his fly open before her father found them.

Charlie was lucky Sergeant Sanchez hadn't shot him. But the Sergeant had told his father, who'd given him a whipping and a lecture about good girls like Juliana. And her father had sent her away. Charlie hadn't seen her since.

Right now he felt just like he'd felt back then—aching with unfulfilled lust and regret.

"Look what the cat dragged in." His brother Rick's voice broke through his reverie.

Charlie jerked in surprise. He rose and approached the bars, his heart pounding hard in his chest. It took all his acting ability to play it cool. He'd dreaded this meeting for two years. Did his brother think the wrong brother had died? "I didn't know you were home."

"I didn't know you were either." Rick had the same dark brown hair as him, but cropped close to his head, and their father's brown eyes. He was thirty-four, four years older than Charlie, and built like a football player, like their dad.

"I flew in last night." Charlie kept his tone light. "How'd you know I was here?"

"The desk sergeant called me. What the hell were you thinking? Solicitation?" Rick spat the last word.

"I'm on a case. I was trying to get information."

"You're an actor, Charlie."

Charlie shook his head. He blamed himself for their two-year estrangement. "I gave it up."

Rick snorted. "When? You wanted to be an actor your whole life."

"I wasn't very good at it. I got tired of bit parts, four am wake-up calls, and working three jobs to pay the rent. Now people pay me to find things for them."

Rick glared at him. "C'mon, pull the other one. You'd sooner quit breathing than give up acting."

Charlie shrugged. That had been true once. Before Billy died. "Fine. Don't believe me."

"Have you seen Mom and Dad?"

Charlie looked away. "No. I told you I'm on a case. I didn't know I was going to be in town."

"Are you going to see them?"

Charlie smiled and tapped the bars. "I'm locked up at the moment."

"Still a funny man. Listen, you should see Mom and Dad while you're here. I'll call them and—"

"No!" Charlie tried to control his breathing. He couldn't face his parents yet, especially not while he was in jail. He was still building his business, and he wanted them to see him successful.

Rick used his cop stare on him, but Charlie had grown up with it, had watched it perfected. It had no effect.

"Are you avoiding something, bro?" Rick demanded.

A lot of things. "I can't waste my client's time for personal matters, Rick. He needs his property back. And sitting around in this cell isn't getting me any closer to retrieving it."

"You haven't been home in two years. It's hard to believe you couldn't spare a few days in all that time."

"New business owners have to work sixty hours a week or more. We don't get time off. And right now it's only me, so even when I'm not on a case, there's paperwork, billing, paying bills, soliciting work. And then there's the mundane personal stuff like laundry and groceries."

"I get it," Rick growled. "It doesn't have anything to do with avoiding Billy's grave."

Charlie was proud of how he controlled his flinch. Billy's death was a wound that wouldn't heal. But Charlie hadn't been an actor all those years without learning something about his craft. "I dealt with his death two years ago." When he'd changed his life. "I swear on his grave I'm on a case."

Rick sighed. "I don't understand it, but I believe you."

"How long have you been back, Rick?"

"Four months."

"And how long 'til you get antsy and leave again?"

Rick's lips quirked into a funny, silly smile. It unnerved Charlie. "I turned down a chance last week. My *wife* didn't want to move."

Charlie's world rocked on its ear. "Wife? When did you get married?"

Rick looked smug. "Two months ago." Then he sobered. "I called to invite you but you didn't answer. I left you a message."

Charlie would have remembered a call like that, but he hadn't been checking his home answering machine much. "Sorry. I told you I'm building my business." Rick looked ready to argue, so he said, "Tell me about the woman who nailed your feet to Miami."

He listened in amazement to the brother who'd pursued evidence and facts his whole life describe his wife, Analise, who allegedly saw and spoke to ghosts. And Charlie had thought there were strange people in California.

"She made me take dance lessons." Rick grimaced. "So we can dance with two of the ghosts during the full moon. It's hard not to run into the girls, since I can't see them. I try to read their location from where Analise is, but I'm wrong a lot. I hate how it feels when they float through me." He shuddered and gripped his stomach. "Analise says it's because I'm very sensitive to spiritual energy."

Charlie gaped. He could not believe the words coming out of Rick's mouth.

"But I love Analise. That's our deal—if I accept the ghosts, she'll live with me. I can't wait for you to meet her. You're going to love her. You'll love our dog, Fitz, too."

Rick had settled down with a wife and a dog. He didn't seem troubled by Billy's death or unsolved murder. Maybe when Charlie's business was a success, Billy's death would stop haunting him.

CHAPTER 2

Juliana limped into the precinct behind Hector and their latest catch—a self-proclaimed preacher she recognized from television. He had an adoring wife and two young children. Juliana felt disgusted to have collared him.

When she reached the squad room, she pulled up short. Charlie Ziffkin sat on the edge of her vice friend's desk, his leg swinging, the right side of his mouth quirked up in a sexy smile.

She reached for calm. "How'd you get out?"

His smile turned smug. "With the truth, of course. It opens every door. My story checked out."

She limped closer. "That's impossible."

Charlie cocked his head. He looked so sexy, darn him. "Have you lived with me all these years that you know me so well?"

"I've seen your name in movie credits. I know you're an actor."

"Lately?"

Juliana had to think. "Last year."

"It sometimes takes eighteen months to get a movie out."

She had no answer to that. Charlie was a natural actor, a real chameleon. Why would he give it up? It made no sense. She lifted the phone and called the booking clerk.

"Why did you release Charlie Ziffkin? He was brought in for solicitation."

"His story checked out. He's got a valid California P.I. license. He's got a California business named Hollywood Investigations for which he files taxes with the IRS. The business has a website with testimonials on it. His brother in homicide came and talked to him. He swears he believes the story."

"Thanks, Hernandez." Unbelievable. She stared at Charlie, trying to figure out how he could be a P.I. "He says your brother vouched for you."

"I bet that's not all he said. I never lied to you, Juliana." Charlie hopped off the desk, took her hand, and guided her into a chair. "What did you do to your ankle?" He stroked her flesh. His touch made her shiver.

"It's not my ankle. It's these damn shoes."

He fought a smile. "If Sister Mary Margaret could see you now."

She unbuckled her shoes then yanked them off. When she lifted her head, Charlie's gaze was riveted to her cleavage. She glanced down and saw that only her areoles were covered. Her face flamed, but the heat in his eyes made her lower body throb with need.

"My mind boggles to see a good Catholic girl working vice," he drawled.

"I'm not a cop. I'm filling in for their regular detective who got food poisoning."

"So this isn't the way you usually dress?" He waved at her outfit.

"The top isn't mine."

"Oh yes it is."

Her nipples peaked. He noticed.

"Charlie …"

"What time do you get off?" Charlie's eyes darkened.

She was sure hers did, too. She remembered his weight on her, his eager fumbling before they'd been interrupted.

"We never finished what we started." His statement sounded like an enticement.

Juliana licked dry lips. "No we didn't."

"Aren't you curious what it would feel like?"

Oh, God, yes! She'd wanted to feel him inside her when she was sixteen; she felt the same need now. "I still have my Catholic school uniform. It's a little tight, though."

"God, I've fantasized about that uniform for years." His eyes were blue flames surrounding an expanding core of black. He waited, apparently leaving it up to her.

All Juliana knew about him now was he claimed to have given up acting to be a private detective. The boy she'd known would never have done that. But her memories of him included him peering through a magnifying glass pretending to be Sherlock Holmes, with her the ever-faithful Watson by his side. He'd played Batman; she'd been Robin. Maybe for him the line between fantasy and reality had blurred.

Yet outwardly he seemed so familiar. His hair still fell in waves, just as she'd admired as a girl. His dimple flashed, and she melted. Apparently puppy love never died. He was still Charlie. The only time he'd ever been completely serious was when he'd been poised above her all those years ago. She wanted to finish what they'd started.

"Come home with me." Before she could change her mind, she wrote directions and her cell phone number on a piece of paper and handed it to him. She could eliminate this one regret from her life.

"You'll wear your school uniform? That is hot," he waved at her getup, "but that uniform … "

"I'll wear it." Her voice sounded breathy, like the teenager she'd been.

"Good." Charlie slid his hand down her arm and intertwined their fingers.

The familiar tingling sensation, that she'd "found" something, startled her. Did he have an item on him that was lost or—her breath caught—stolen? But he'd touched her twice before this and her psychic alarm hadn't sounded either of those times. He hadn't picked up anything in the past few minutes. Why was she sensing something now?

"I'll follow you," Charlie said, not sensing anything unusual. No one ever did.

"Sure." She'd get him naked and go over his clothes with a fine-toothed comb. Well, after she made love to him.

She drove home in a blur of lust. Her panties were damp by the time she reached her second-floor apartment. Her nipples were taut to the point of pain. Her pussy felt empty and achy.

Charlie followed her inside, crowding against her, his flesh hot against hers. The lock clicked under her fingers. She took hold of his hand and fought the tingling sensation. Later.

Her apartment flew by in a blur of colors as she tugged him into her bedroom and released him next to the bed. It took a moment to search her closet, but then she pulled out her old school uniform. She didn't know why she'd kept it all these years. She'd hated the all-girl religious high school.

But then she looked at the hunger on Charlie's face, so much like the expression he'd worn that fateful day years ago, and she knew why she'd kept it. Because of him.

Charlie removed his black suit jacket. His shoulders were wider, his chest deeper. As she removed the skirt and blouse from the hanger, he tugged the sleeveless maroon vest over his head.

She paused, savoring how hot he looked in his black T-shirt and jeans. With his mussed, collar-length, wavy hair and beard stubble, he looked disreputable—a bad boy. And she was going to be a bad girl.

"Why'd you stop?" he asked.

"I wanted to savor how you've changed. You've grown."

"Yeah, I have." His husky voice sounded sexy. His arousal strained against his pants.

Juliana laid the uniform on her bedroom chair and reached for the hem of her tight shirt. Charlie watched, which made her feel even wickeder. Bit by bit she tugged it up, peeling it off her flesh. It took a lot of wriggling, but finally she was free and tossed it away.

Sweat dotted Charlie's face. He licked his lips. "That was quite an appetizer."

"I'm not done yet." She found the hidden zipper in the tight denim skirt and tugged it down. Once more she had to shimmy, gyrating back and forth. Kicking the skirt away, she stood in her red satin bra and panties.

"God," Charlie croaked. "You'd make a fortune as an exotic dancer."

"I only do private dances." She swallowed. "You're overdressed."

"So I am." He dragged the T-shirt over his head with no fanfare. Her gaze followed the sparse black hair from his tight brown nipples down his firm chest past his washboard abs to where it disappeared into his jeans. He looked damn good in those jeans.

"You want me to leave them on?" He indicated his jeans. "So it'll be like it was back then?"

"No." She shook her head. "We're going all the way this time."

"Man, wait'll I tell the guys at school." He smiled, then unzipped his jeans and dropped them to the floor.

Oh, he was a bad boy. Black cotton cupped him, lovingly outlining his straining cock.

Juliana picked up the short plaid skirt and stepped into it. As she eased it up over her hips, she breathed a sigh of relief. It still fit. She zipped it closed.

When she reached for her bra clasp, Charlie exclaimed, "What are you doing?"

"I need to take this off in order to get the blouse on. It's a push-up bra."

"I think I want to see what it does for that blouse."

Juliana slipped her arms into it. When she tried to button it, she could only get the bottom buttons closed. It gapped, displaying her cleavage like a dessert offering. She looked like a porn actress.

But one glance at Charlie told her the outfit achieved the desired effect.

"Do you have the knee socks?" he croaked.

"Of course." She sat on the bed and pulled them on. She made sure Charlie got a good view of her damp panties.

Then she stood. They were ready to finish the scene begun more than a dozen years ago.

Charlie licked his lips. "Right. What position were we in back then?"

"Why don't we start from the beginning?"

"That's a better idea. Come here, Juliana."

She was thrilled, yet nervous. This was Charlie, but a new-and-improved Charlie with unknown qualities. She moved to stand in front of him.

"What do you want, little Jules?" He'd used his nickname for her on that day, even though he'd known what she wanted.

"Make me a woman, Chaz."

"I can see you're very much a woman now." He traced a finger over the mounds of her breasts, just above her areoles. Her nipples pinched to tight points. Her pussy tightened.

He covered her breasts with both hands. There was no fumbled groping. This Charlie knew how to handle a woman. "These want to come out to see me, don't they?"

"Oh, yes."

Charlie dipped his hands into her tight bra. Juliana sucked in her breath. As soon as his fingers brushed her nipples she gasped.

"Easy." His fingers stroked her aching nipples.

Juliana groaned. She strained into his touch. He rubbed harder. She gripped his biceps.

"Harder, Charlie."

For a moment the pressure increased, then he exclaimed with frustration. "It's difficult with this bra."

"Here." She moved her hands to her shirt.

But Charlie stopped her. "This is *my* fantasy." He dipped his hands back into her bra and released her breasts.

Juliana sighed with relief as Charlie covered her breasts with his hands. She stood on tiptoe so he could have better access. He thumbed her nipples until she groaned.

"You should see how you look," he said, his voice husky. "Your breasts are beautiful. They're fuller than they were."

"I'm a late bloomer."

"I love how they feel." Charlie rubbed her nipples between his thumbs and forefingers.

Juliana's panties were soaked, her pussy clenching in anticipation.

"I need to taste them," he rumbled.

"Yes!"

Charlie gently pushed her on the bed and then followed her down. He eased his body between her legs. Then he took her left nipple into his hot mouth and suckled. Juliana cried out. He pressed his cock against her aching cleft. She thrust her body against him.

He was skilled with his mouth and his hands. Neither of them had known what to do back then. Now they did, although she wished they'd learned together.

She writhed with pleasure, arching her back to force her breast deeper into his mouth. He obliged by sucking hard. She thrashed her head. Her nails gripped his shoulders. He flicked and pinched and nipped her nipple. He rubbed his cotton-covered penis repeatedly across her aching body.

Tension gripped her lower belly. Her nipples throbbed. Pleasure streaked to her pussy. She ached. Her orgasm built. She cried out and pressed herself to him until the pleasure released her.

Juliana looked up into Charlie's eyes. Only a narrow ring of bright blue remained.

"I need to get a condom."

She nodded, although she didn't want him to leave her.

Charlie climbed off the bed and bent down for his jeans. What those black cotton briefs did for him was pure sin.

He turned and stopped, staring at her. "My God, you look so hot."

He stripped off the black briefs. His cock was full and thick with arousal. Tearing open the package with violent motions, he sheathed himself. Here was another difference from that first time. Protection hadn't even entered their minds.

Charlie climbed on the bed between her legs. Juliana opened wide to receive him. When he leaned down, she made a sound of protest. She still had her panties on!

But Charlie's head kept descending and she realized he meant to kiss her. Shock kept her pliant under his warm, firm lips. She'd never kissed him before. They'd tried to have sex as teenagers, too eager for the act to savor the preliminaries.

Tonight she hadn't expected … well, she'd expected to get laid.

His lips felt so marvelous against hers she had to respond. She'd never had a kiss feel this wonderful. She threw herself into it wholeheartedly, gripping Charlie's back, and ate him up like a greedy girl with an ice cream cone. Chocolate mint. He ate her, too. His tongue licked hers like a lover's stroke. They kissed until they were both breathless.

Charlie broke away to demand, "Who taught you how to kiss like this?"

"You did. Just now." Juliana dragged him back for more.

He sucked her down into a vortex of exquisite wonder. His mouth was a pleasure land, his lips instruments of seduction.

"We have to do this," he gasped. "I can barely hold on."

"Make love to me, Charlie."

He nearly tore her panties off. Then he was back and she felt his hot flesh against her. She raised her hips and in one exquisite plunge he filled her. Juliana went rigid, gasping. Her entire body tingled with her "finder" senses. What the hell? She gripped him to her hard and ignored the psychic sensation.

"Don't move," she begged. He felt so right inside her.

"Did I hurt you? Were you a virgin?" Charlie's voice rose with incredulity.

"No. I'm all right, and I wasn't a virgin. Just hold still."

Charlie froze. His body tensed. "What is it?"

"We fit perfectly." She heard the amazement in her voice. But he filled her like none of her other lovers had. She was gripped with the feeling of rightness, of coming home.

"You feel so good I gotta move." Charlie sounded like he was in pain.

Juliana wanted to move, too, so she did, raising her hips to his until her mound was pressed hard to his pubic bone.

He groaned with pleasure. He began slow, but soon it wasn't enough, and his thrusts grew hard and urgent. Juliana thrust with him.

The tension built and built, until she couldn't take any more. She came and cried out. Charlie groaned hoarsely and came with her. Pressed flesh to flesh, she felt their union couldn't be more perfect.

They collapsed and lay gasping.

Charlie kissed her. "I wish we'd done this back then."

Juliana had thought the same when they started. But she knew the truth now. They couldn't have. Charlie had to be lost in order to find this.

CHAPTER 3

Juliana searched Charlie's belongings while he slept. She turned out every pocket and touched every item in them, but nothing made her hands tingle.

Her psychometry reacted only when she touched *him*.

"Looking for clues?" His groggy voice came from the bed.

Juliana jerked, but then finished what she was doing. She worked with cops, and was a cop's daughter. It was in her blood to be thorough. "I'm just checking."

Charlie sat up. The red sheet pooled in his lap. He looked damn sexy. "You don't believe my story?"

"What story? You didn't tell me anything." She found his wallet, opened it, and looked through his cards. His driver's license and P.I. license were California issue. "Nice photos."

"That's a pretty nice pose yourself."

Juliana wore only her plaid skirt and knee socks. He'd stripped off her blouse and bra the second time they'd made love. She knew kneeling by his clothes was provocative, but she hadn't planned it. Her naked loins tingled and ached for his touch and penetration. Her nipples pearled.

She tried to concentrate even with the heat of his interested gaze on her. His Screen Actors Guild card was tucked away in one of the pockets. Why did he keep it, unless private investigating was just something he was playing at for a while? He'd been like that as a youth. Every few months he wanted to be something else—pirate, pilot, superhero. But he always returned to acting.

Behind that card was an old photo of him and her. They must have been eight or nine. They had their arms around one another and were mugging for the camera. They looked so young and happy together. Her throat felt tight. Why did he keep this photo with him? *You've got more than one.*

She shook off her surprise and concentrated on the task at hand. "What are you really up to, Charlie?"

"Oh, about eight inches."

Juliana looked. She couldn't help it. The sheet tented in his lap. She licked her lips. Her pussy clenched. "I mean what are you doing here in Miami?"

"You mean besides living out my fantasies?"

She nodded, unable to speak.

"I'm tracking a stolen item for a client."

"Why not ask the police for help?"

"And risk losing my finder's fee? No thanks."

Juliana tucked his wallet back in his jacket. It was finely made, good material, great tailoring. It must have cost a lot of money.

"What was stolen?"

"An object."

"Don't play with me, Charlie. I'm serious."

"I assure you I'm deadly serious about what I'm going to do to you." As he rose from the bed the sheet slipped from his body, exposing his erect cock.

He stalked over to her. She stayed on her knees, no longer questioning him. She wanted him again. When he knelt behind her with his hand on her back, she lifted her bottom to him.

"You don't know what you do to me in this skirt." But as he pressed his hard erection inside her, filling her completely, she knew what she did to him.

• • •

Charlie woke with his arms wrapped around a woman and his body spooned so tight against hers his soft cock was inside her. It took only a moment to identify her as Juliana, and instantly his cock hardened and he wanted her again. But he had work to do and not much time to get it done.

Had she been another woman, he could have taken her quickly and eased the burning ache in his cock. But with Juliana he needed more time. It was almost the hardest thing he'd ever done to pull out of her. She murmured a protest, and he nearly succumbed to her lure once more. But her clock showed it was two-fifteen in the morning. He had to talk to Carlos at that bar the hooker had named, and it was nearly closing time.

Charlie dressed quietly and left Juliana's bedroom, giving one last glance at the nude woman barely covered by the red sheet. God, she was beautiful with her long hair tousled by their lovemaking. Anyone looking at this scene would be able to tell she'd been well and truly loved. And yet he still wanted her.

He drove away wishing he had more time in Miami to explore the many facets of Juliana. The sexual ones alone would take weeks. For the umpteenth time tonight, he wished her father hadn't interrupted them all those years ago. They'd have been lovers throughout high school. Then he wouldn't have spent those final years lonely and aching for her.

She'd lived next door to him for ten years, and he hadn't seen her as anything more than his playmate and best friend. Then she'd gotten breasts, and Charlie could hardly think of anything else, not even acting. Right now he was having the same problem. If he turned his car around, he could go back to Juliana's bed and sate himself a few more times. She wouldn't argue.

There was something different about her; something ethereal that hadn't been there when she was a teenager.

Charlie made a quick stop at his hotel to change and pick up his other business cards, the ones that proclaimed him a Hollywood promoter. Thank God he hadn't had them on him when he'd been arrested; otherwise, he would have had a harder time convincing the cops. There were times when pretending he had Hollywood connections opened doors that being a P.I. didn't.

He had to find the sculpture and get back to California before the memories in this town overwhelmed him. And making love to his childhood friend and teenaged crush wasn't helping. It reminded him of how he'd felt the first time someone he'd loved was ripped from his life.

After Sergeant Sanchez had sent Juliana away, Charlie had tried not to moon over her absence. But Rick had teased him without mercy. Luckily his oldest brother, Michael, had already moved out. Only Billy had seemed to understand the depth of hurt Charlie kept hidden. He needed her, not just his best friend. His body ached for what she'd promised him, which was his and his alone. They'd agreed to initiate one another into adulthood, but it hadn't happened.

And someone else had gotten to Juliana first. Charlie's hands curled into fists. He tried to remind himself they were nothing to each other now. They hadn't been best friends in years. They'd fulfilled their unkept promises three times tonight. They owed one another nothing more. They'd both go on to other lovers, and Juliana would marry someone and have his children.

The world went black around him, and a familiar pain gripped his chest, the sense of loss overwhelming. He didn't deserve Juliana. He should be happy with the hours they'd shared in her bed. The memories would have to be enough.

Ruthlessly he squelched his desire. He'd become an expert at doing that. He had a sculpture to find.

• • •

Juliana could tell her father knew about last night's masquerade when he called her at eight in the morning.

"Juliana, I want you in my office in one hour." His tone was curt.

She sighed. "Yes, sir."

A dial tone was his reply.

She replaced the receiver and glanced at the other side of the bed to find it empty. There were no sounds in her apartment, so she knew Charlie had gone. She felt ... disappointed.

Another sigh escaped her. He'd gotten what he'd wanted. She had to be honest with herself—it was what they'd both wanted. She'd been a more than willing participant last night. In fact, she'd like to make love with Charlie a few more times—like now.

She felt the sheet where Charlie had lain and found it cool to her touch. He'd been gone for hours.

Well, no sense mooning over his loss. She swung her legs over the side of the bed and sat up, wincing. That last time had been vigorous to the point of being rough. And she'd loved it.

Juliana rose and headed for the shower. The warm water leached the sensual aches from her body and washed his scent away. But as she studied her naked form in the mirror afterward, she knew nothing could eliminate the whisker burns, the rug burns, the bruises from his fierce hold and the—heaven help her—honest-to-God hickey on her neck. She touched it. When had Charlie done that?

The man had been insatiable. They'd wasted all those hours from the moment she hit puberty when they could have been having mind-blowing sex.

Juliana masked the marks of Charlie's passion the best she could. Her long hair hid most of the hickey, and a long lightweight skirt covered her knees. She didn't like appearing before her father with marks showing. But if he knew about Charlie ... well, what of it? She was twenty-nine, not sixteen. He didn't have any say in her love life.

Still, she had to take in a deep breath and pull her shoulders back before she stepped into Captain Sanchez's office.

"Shut the door," he ordered.

She took this time to swallow. She'd known she was being stupid last night.

Juliana sat in the padded chair in front of his desk and tried not to fidget while he looked her over. Her father was a big man, wide shoulders to go with his six-foot-four frame. He'd let his liberally salted black hair grow out a little and now he swept it back from his forehead. The longer style softened the face that looked like a boxer's with its big broken nose.

"Tell me about last night. What were you thinking going out on that sting?"

Juliana lifted her chin. "I thought that after all their planning it was too bad Marta got food poisoning so she couldn't work."

"They could have found another detective. Marta's not the only female vice cop. *You* didn't have to take her place."

"It was perfectly safe, Papá."

"You don't know that."

"Hector and Karl were with me the whole time. I never went anywhere with the johns."

"You're not a cop, Juliana. We don't use civilians in stings."

"I'm more than a civilian, Papá."

His face flushed with anger. "You knew it was wrong to go. Why did you do it?"

Juliana didn't know if she could explain. "I don't feel like I do enough to help. It's not like I find people. I thought when I started working with the police I'd feel, I don't know, useful. But I don't."

Her father's face gentled. "*Chica*, we only use you on the hardest cases, the ones we can't solve with regular police work."

"But why do you have to try regular methods first? I've got an 85% success rate at finding things."

"You know why. The public pays us to do the job. They won't pay a psychic. There's a reason we keep your assistance as quiet as possible. Well, two reasons."

"You're protecting me." She was tired of being cosseted.

"You're all I have left of your mama."

"I'm fully grown, *Dad*." On purpose she used the English word. "You can't keep protecting me my whole life."

He glowered. He didn't like her stepping outside the role of dutiful Latina daughter. "I'm a cop, it's what I do. And I'm your *papá*. That's what papás do."

Juliana sighed. He was never going to get past the car accident that had killed her mother and injured her. If only she was brave enough to move far away, like Charlie had. But she'd lost both the dreams that would give her the courage—being a cop and loving Charlie. *He returned*, the thought teased. But he wouldn't stay.

Her father blew out his breath. "I heard they caught Charlie Ziffkin in the sting."

Juliana's cheeks burned. She adjusted her hair forward around her neck. "Yeah. He's all grown up, too."

His dark eyes bored into her. "They kicked him loose."

She shrugged with feigned carelessness. "He said he was a P.I. on a case. His brother believed him."

"Last I heard he was an actor in Hollywood."

So he'd been following Charlie's life? "That's what I thought, too."

"Did he say anything to you, *m'hija*?"

"Like what?" Juliana tried to look innocent.

He studied her. The hickey burned like a brand. She tried not to fidget.

"*Chica*, I did what I thought was best sending you to your Aunt Dolores until I could sell the house. I didn't want you pregnant and unmarried. You had your whole life ahead of you."

"I know, Papá." But he wouldn't let her live her life.

"Thank God I did, seeing how young Ziffkin turned out."

Juliana tried not to think about how she and Charlie had consummated their thirteen-year separation. "He lives in California, Papá. I don't think you need to worry about him." *Or me ever seeing him again.* A pain stabbed her chest in the vicinity of her heart.

"Good. You'll be happy to know another department has asked for your help."

She sat up, electrified. "A case?"

"Yes. It's rather odd. It's narcotics."

She deflated. "You know I have little success finding drugs."

"Yes, well they don't need you to find drugs. I'll let them tell you about it." He held out a piece of paper, and she took it. "Go to the Fourth Precinct and ask for Detective Montoya in Narcotics."

"All right." She frowned. It was odd that her father was being so closed-mouthed. But she rose, stuffing the paper in her purse. She made it to the door before her father spoke again.

"Juliana, there's a love bite on your neck."

She couldn't control her jerk of unwelcome surprise. She dared not look at him or answer because anything she said could incriminate her.

"I know you're an adult living on your own … " He stuttered to a stop. "I think I'd like to meet the young man."

Oh, God. She moistened her lips. "Papá, you make young men nervous."

"Only if they have something they wish to hide. Does this young man have something to hide?"

Only a one-night stand with his daughter. Only the name Charlie Ziffkin. She lifted her chin and turned to face him. She was not a child. "When the time is right, you'll meet the man who's important to me."

Her father tried to stare her into submission, but she'd worked too hard fighting his tight control to back down.

"I hope it's soon, *m'hija*."

Juliana escaped, breathing a great sigh of relief. It wouldn't be soon.

Detective Joaquin Montoya in Narcotics looked the part—early thirties, dark hair in waves to his shoulders, dressed in black jeans, a loose colorful shirt, and a chunky gold necklace.

His partner, Brian Hunt, was grungy with straight dishwater blond hair. He was thin enough to pass as a teenager, but the hard edge to his gaze revealed he was much older.

They took her to one of the interrogation rooms and closed the door. Montoya gestured for her to take a seat. He fidgeted, so she knew what was coming and braced herself to face a nonbeliever.

"I don't believe in psychics," he began.

"Then why am I here?" She'd heard it dozens of times before.

"What we're looking for is out of the ordinary. We've tried regular ways to find it. Nothing has worked so far." Montoya scowled and glanced at his partner. "If you weren't Captain Sanchez's daughter—"

Juliana held up her hand. "Stop right there. I don't help the department because I'm his daughter, and I don't listen to requests because he's a captain. That has nothing to do with this. Facts are facts. I have a high success rate at recovering things that are missing."

Montoya's bronze face flushed, but whether in shame or anger, Juliana couldn't tell.

"We need to find this item." Detective Hunt's cold mask had dropped. "It's very important and will prevent a flood of drugs coming into Miami."

"Why don't you tell me what you know," she suggested.

Hunt looked at Montoya, and then leaned forward on the metal table. "We have a reliable snitch. He says there's excitement in the drug distribution community. There's going to be a new pipeline of cocaine established, but who gets to head the pipeline depends on who locates an item the Columbian drug lord wants."

"What item?" she asked, intrigued.

Montoya shrugged. "Some relic supposed to have special significance to the Columbian."

"You can't stop it from being brought into the country?"

"It's already here. In fact, the snitch is sure it's in Miami," Hunt answered.

"And you want me to find it." Juliana inhaled. "I'm not sure I can help. I need something related to the item to draw me to it."

The detectives looked at one another. She saw doubt on Montoya's face. "We don't have anything related to it."

"Do you have a photo? Sometimes that works."

"No." Montoya scowled.

"Then I'm sorry, detectives, but I can't help you." She rose.

"I told you it was a waste of time," Montoya growled to his partner.

Detective Hunt held out his hand. "I'm sorry we wasted your time."

Juliana shook it. When he released her, something warm and slippery slid into her palm. She closed her fist to keep the object from falling.

Juliana saw the dead girl, needle tracks stark on her stick-thin arms. Her long, blonde hair was unwashed and unkempt. A necklace hung around her pale neck.

As the vision faded, Juliana asked Hunt, "Who is she?"

"Lila." His gaze was intent.

Montoya's head snapped around to stare at his partner.

"You wear her necklace," Juliana realized. "It's warm from your body." She closed her eyes and knew three more things instantly. "Lila was your sister. You became a narc because she OD'd."

When she opened her eyes, Hunt was nodding. He didn't look surprised. But Montoya's mouth hung open. Juliana ignored him and handed the necklace to Hunt. "You wanted your partner to know I was real."

"Yeah. He can be closed-minded," Hunt said with smug satisfaction.

"Bite me," Montoya retorted.

"I still can't help you without something related to the object. Get me that and I'll do what I can. You said it was a relic. Do you know where it came from? Are there other items from that same location?"

Montoya shook his head. "We don't even know what kind of relic it is. We'll ask our snitch to get more information."

Juliana gave him her business card. "Contact me directly next time."

She turned to his partner. "Detective Hunt, will you walk me out?"

Hunt frowned but followed her out of the department. When they were alone in the corridor, he said, "I assume you want to say more about the necklace?"

Juliana swallowed and nodded. "Your lady, Celeste, doesn't understand why you wear another woman's chain."

Detective Hunt was unable to hide his surprise.

"Perhaps you've worn it long enough."

She left it at that and drove home to her apartment. Maybe she should take her own advice. She'd mooned over Charlie for long enough. Now that she'd had him, she could let the dream Charlie go.

Unfortunately, now that she'd had him, she wanted him even more.

CHAPTER 4

Charlie wore the scent of sex all day. It had been a mistake not to shower after leaving Juliana's bed. It was so strong it overpowered him at every turn, swamping him in carnal memories of Juliana's breasts, the glistening pink flesh between her legs, and her tight body gloving him as he thrust.

He didn't know how he had had any coherency to talk to dozens of people and keep his cover story straight. But he had, and he felt elated to have a lead. Rumor said a new major narcotics dealer would soon emerge. The details of how this would happen were murky, but it involved a bidding war and a relic. The reward for having this relic was to operate a new drug pipeline to Columbia. Rumor said the relic was in town. It had to be the sculpture, crazy as that sounded.

The people he'd talked to agreed there were only a few men powerful enough to pit Miami's drug dealers against one another in a bidding war and live. All Charlie had to do was find out which man it was and steal the sculpture back before the auction began.

Something bothered him about the whole thing, so he stopped in the local library to view their newspaper archives and do a landline Internet search. He didn't want to risk a wireless search on his laptop.

Charlie's client, Hollywood promoter Jordan Hessler, had told him the sculpture was the fertility god Hun-apu. Why would a sculpture of a fertility god be of interest to a drug lord?

He did a search for Hun-apu and found the Maya Hero Twins Hunahpu and Xbalanque. The photo of the sculpture Jordan had given him and the one on the computer screen matched. What he'd thought was a man and woman was actually twin brothers. The twins had outwitted gods and the lords of the Mayan underworld, defeating their enemies through trickery and great powers. But those powers didn't include fertility.

He sat back in the chair, exhaling. Someone had the crazy idea this sculpture was mystical or something and thought it valuable enough to trade it for a drug route. It sounded insane. He'd had some superstitions in his acting life and had known other actors who did, too, but they wouldn't put stock in mystical sculptures.

That thought made him frown. Hessler had said the sculpture increased his libido fourfold and he had to have it back to satisfy his young new girlfriend who'd given it to him. But someone else thought it was more valuable than that … or had *known* it was.

What a bizarre coincidence that someone knew Hessler had the sculpture.

Charlie turned that over in his mind. Maybe Hessler's girlfriend had told someone she'd smuggled the sculpture into the country. There weren't a lot of secrets on a movie location. And the drug community seemed to be insidious. It wouldn't be hard to learn her secret.

But if the sculpture was so valuable to drug dealers, why didn't the California dealers seize it? Why drag it to Miami? None of this made sense.

It was more likely the sculpture contained contraband of some kind—like diamonds. Charlie shook his head to dispel the images. His imagination was out of control. He started a newspaper archive search on the names of the powerful Miami men he'd been given.

The first, Humberto Estrada, was an import-export mogul, which Charlie thought the perfect front for moving drugs. Estrada had a mansion in Miami Beach, with direct access on the water. He was a ruthless businessman with a growing hold on import-export. He'd increased the size of his empire after the mysterious death of a competitor several months ago. Charlie's brother, Michael, owned a successful small business in that industry. He felt a pang of regret that he couldn't ask his brother about Estrada. *Later.* When he'd proven himself to his family.

The second man, Dalton Montgomery, was new money. He'd been rumored to be part of Stefan Carmana's crime organization until that man's death—Charlie suffered a jolt of surprise—after being shot by Detective Richard Ziffkin two months ago. Carmana had been attempting to murder Analise Angelloti when he was killed. That had to be Rick's wife. Chills ran up Charlie's spine.

Montgomery seemed to have his hand in a lot of things, including construction, tourism, yachts, and luxury condos. His daughter, recently graduated from Miami University, was engaged to be married to old money … this weekend. What a perfect place for drug dealers to mingle and no one would be the wiser. Charlie made a note to get a look at the guest list. It would be easier to slip into Montgomery's South Beach mansion during the wedding preparations and look around for the sculpture.

The last man on the list, Michael Scarvelis, was in real estate, with property all over Florida. He held numerous social events at his mansion in North Bay.

With all the gala events the three men held, there were plenty of photos of their properties, and it didn't take Charlie long to find the addresses. Unfortunately, the only one entertaining a large group in the next week was Montgomery.

Charlie printed the articles about the Montgomery wedding. He now knew the names of the florist, the caterer, the photographer, and the wedding planner. And in a few more minutes, he found their addresses and phone numbers. He loved the Internet.

While he was online, Charlie also Googled Juliana. What he found blew him away. The few articles about her called her a psychic who could find lost or stolen things. *Stolen things.* He couldn't believe it; after all, they'd played together as children.

He'd almost made love to the teenaged Juliana. He *had* made love to the woman. She wasn't a psychic.

But there were several newspaper articles where she'd worked with the Miami PD to recover stolen goods. She'd led the cops to a valuable painting, a diamond necklace, and a yacht. She told the interviewer she noticed her ability after the car accident that injured her and killed her mother, that sometimes head injuries precipitated psychic abilities in a person. Hers was named *psychometry*.

Charlie's breath sighed out of him. She'd been quieter after the accident, different. He'd thought it was grief. He hadn't known what to say to her. And then she'd offered him his heart's desire.

Last night he'd labeled that difference ethereal. But he'd bet it was because she was psychic. He looked up psychometry and found out these psychics could hold an object to learn more about it or a person connected to it. He clicked back to the article about her. He touched her photo. He'd thought her pretty as a teenager. He found her beautiful now.

And she was exactly what he needed. In more ways than one. He tried to crush thoughts of sating himself in her body. He didn't need more heartache knowing he couldn't keep her. Now that he knew she was even more special, he knew he wasn't enough for her. But his lower body had a mind of its own, and his hard-on throbbed with his thoughts of getting laid.

Dammit. There was a phone number for her in the article. Charlie wrote it down. Then he collected his printed sheets and exited the building to make a call.

Juliana being psychic was like fate. But fate would have to wait. Charlie got her voice mail and left a message. Then he drove to his hotel to wash the fading scent of sex off him. He couldn't help hoping to renew the scent once more.

His cell phone was ringing when he stepped out of the shower. He snatched it and a towel. "Hollywood Investigations."

"Charlie?"

The sound of his name in her husky voice gave him an immediate hard-on. "Yeah."

"You need my help finding the object you're looking for?"

"Yeah. I didn't know you could do that. I found articles about you when I was researching my case today."

"Why don't you come over and we can talk about it."

His horny self read all kinds of things into her statement. "Sure. I can be there in twenty minutes."

"Do you have something related to it or a photo of the item?"

"I've got a photo."

"Bring it and I'll see what I can do."

"I'm coming." God, he hoped that was prophetic.

• • •

Juliana wiped her palms on her skirt before she opened the front door. Once again Charlie's sexy looks took her breath away. She hadn't thought she'd see him again, yet here he was. His midnight blue striped shirt deepened the cerulean of his eyes. He wore dark slacks and dress shoes. He'd shaved, so now the intriguing dimple in his chin showed, but she missed the disreputable stubble. His dark hair curled with the same unruly waves she remembered from childhood. He looked hot.

"Hi." She felt achy all over. Had it only been a few hours ago that he was riding her and she was begging him to make her come? Moisture pooled between her legs.

"Hi." A sexy little smile tugged at one side of his mouth, and his eyes gleamed.

She remembered his mouth on hers and on other parts of her body. She licked her lips. His gaze zeroed in on the movement. God, she didn't know how she was supposed to conduct business with the man who'd given her the greatest pleasure ever.

"Can I come in?" he asked, his voice smoky.

Oh, God, yes. Had she said that aloud? Her body begged to be stripped, mounted, pleasured, and satisfied. Again and again.

Charlie moved forward. She thought he meant to fulfill her hopefully unvoiced desires. But he shepherded her from the doorway and closed the door behind him.

They were alone in private, both consenting adults. *Get a grip, girl.* "I don't usually meet my clients here," she babbled.

"Where do you meet them?"

"Mostly at the police station. Sometimes in my father's office."

"Thank God he's not here," Charlie said with fervor.

"It's too late for him to stop us this time." Juliana felt like clapping a hand over her mouth. She hadn't planned to discuss what they'd done last night.

"Far too late," Charlie agreed, his voice husky. His blue eyes were like a swimming pool; she wanted to sink into them. Oh, wait, she wanted him to sink into *her*.

"Any regrets?" he asked.

"Oh, no. That was long overdue." Had she said that aloud?

"I agree. You won't have any trouble working with me, will you?"

"No, not at all." Not if you discounted carnal fantasies, shortness of breath, and a heartbeat gone haywire. Oh, and throbbing, aching breasts, a tightening deep in her abdomen, and the compulsive desire to strip Charlie naked and have her wanton way with him.

"I really need this," he said.

"What?" Had he read her mind? She stopped beside the couch.

"Finding the sculpture could open all kinds of doors for me in Hollywood."

Oh, that need. "Why don't we get comfortable?" She did *not* mean anything by that statement.

Charlie's pupils expanded. "Whatever you want."

Juliana's mouth dried. Her body's moisture rushed south. What she wanted … wasn't realistic. She'd let Charlie test-drive her. It's what he'd wanted, what they'd both wanted. He wasn't here for another spin, despite his husky voice and darkened eyes.

But if he touched her, she'd be lost. She'd let him do whatever he wanted with her, as many times as he wanted. She knew she'd deny him nothing. She was his for the taking.

The moment elongated as she waited for Charlie's move, not daring to breathe.

But when he made it, it was to sit on the couch and pull out a photo. Juliana released her breath and sat beside him. She was *not* disappointed. Maybe if she told herself that enough times she'd believe it.

Charlie handed her the photo and immediately she felt a tingling sensation. Her hand had brushed his, so she wasn't sure if it was him or the photo. She scooted further away from him on the cushion and stared at the sculpture.

It looked old, like a stone carving, and was flat, which surprised her. When Charlie had said a sculpture she'd envisioned something three dimensional, but this was two. There were two garish seated figures wearing monstrous elaborate masks and headdresses and little else. It was primitive.

"What is this?" she asked.

"It's a sculpture of the Mayan gods Hunahpu and Xbalanque, the Maya Hero Twins."

"It looks old."

"I don't know if it is or not. My client's girlfriend obtained it in South America when she was filming a movie."

"Tomb raiding?"

"I don't know. She's an actress. Lots of opportunities get offered to actors on movie sets. Maybe someone sold it to her. Or maybe she bought it in a village. It could be a clever reproduction. She told my client it was a fertility god." His smile blazed.

Juliana was distracted by that smile and her curiosity about Charlie's life in California. "Were you offered opportunities on sets?"

He sobered. "Yeah. Drugs, sex, other things. I wasn't a big star, so I didn't get huge enticements, but they were enough to get anybody into trouble."

"Did you get into trouble?"

His sexy smile was wickedly sinful. "Yeah, but not that kind. My family kept me out of most of it. Billy and my parents mostly. And work."

"I thought I'd seen all the movies you were in. I must have missed a lot of them if you were that busy."

Charlie shook his head, his blue eyes sad. "Not acting. Jobs that paid the rent like busboy, waiter, studio model, canvasser, things like that."

"But you wanted to be an actor your whole life."

"So do thousands of other people who flock to California every year. Roles don't get cast based on who wants to be an actor the most."

"But you were good!"

"Thanks for the support. I need to retrieve this sculpture so I can get back to California. Would you see if you can locate it?"

Juliana sensed something beneath Charlie's easy smile. The Charlie she'd grown up with wouldn't have let overwhelming odds stop him. But she followed his lead and picked up the photo. A picture of a large white house filled her mind. It was a mansion surrounded by palm trees, which described a lot of properties in Florida.

"It's a very large white house, two stories at least, maybe three. There's a large pool in the back, shaped like a four leaf clover, a pool house or guesthouse, lots of property." She tried to see more details.

"Can you get an address?" Charlie asked.

She shook her head and laid the photo on the coffee table. "It doesn't work like that. I've got a map of Miami. I'll try to pinpoint it for you."

"If you had a picture of the house, could you tell?"

"Maybe. You have a photo?"

He nodded. "In the car. I'll be right back." Charlie rose and slipped out the door.

Juliana almost wished it wasn't this easy to find the sculpture. She'd like more time to get to know this sexy man again. But he was itching to return to his life in California. She had no right to hold him back. What they'd shared was in the past. Puppy love didn't last.

CHAPTER 5

Excitement urged Charlie back to Juliana's apartment with his file folder of precious photos. If she could pinpoint the sculpture's location, he might be home by tomorrow, away from his family … and her.

That little white top she wore bared a delectable midriff. And the long crinkled melon-colored skirt draped low enough on her abdomen to give him carnal ideas about pulling it down her hips. He wondered what she wore underneath it, if anything. The desire to run his hands up her shapely calves and thighs to find out drove him wild.

He thanked God he'd worn loose black pants; otherwise his hard-on would make it painful to move. He shouldn't make love with her again. That wasn't his reason for being here. He should stick to business.

Juliana looked up when he stepped through the door and all his good intentions dived straight toward hell. Her dark eyes were nearly all pupil. His cock hardened even more. It made him hot to see a woman who desired him as much as Juliana did.

Charlie sucked in several breaths as he fought the urge to pull her down onto his cock. Surrounded by the warmth and color of Mexican fabrics and homemade pots, she burned with Latin life and passion. He needed that passion.

Focus, man.

He approached the couch where she sat watching him like a cat watched its next meal. Careful not to touch her, he sat down and laid the three grainy black-and-white prints from the Internet on the coffee table in front of her.

Juliana reached out, and her palm hovered over the first photo. With her other hand she picked up the photo of the stolen sculpture. She placed her palm on the photo. Charlie held his breath. He noticed by her outthrust breasts that Juliana did, too.

A little frown creased her forehead. "I don't get anything from this one."

She lifted her hand and moved it to the next photo, where she repeated her performance. He held his breath again. "Not this one either."

Juliana moved her hand to the final photo, where she hesitated. "I don't always get something from photos."

"I understand."

Still she hesitated, and he glanced up. Juliana looked at him, not at the pictures. "Charlie, what are you going to do if I tell you it's at this last house?"

"Get it back."

"You mean steal it?"

He smiled. "How can it be stealing when the sculpture doesn't belong to them?"

"Charlie, I mean it. I'm a cop's daughter. I can't help you break the law."

"How is helping me different from helping the police?"

"You're not the law."

"I'm who people turn to when they can't go to the police. My client doesn't want to involve them, and he doesn't want his property tied up for months or years in the legal system."

"You really hire yourself out to find things?"

His mouth quirked up on the right side. "Like you. I get a finder's fee. What do you get?"

"The same. And the satisfaction of catching criminals. It's the only way I can."

Charlie caught the bitter note in her voice. "You could become a cop like your father."

Juliana snorted. "No, I can't. The accident saw to that."

He'd seen every inch of her luscious body. He hadn't seen any impediment to her becoming a police officer. "I don't understand."

"It's this." She spread her hands over the table. "This ability I have. My father told me you can't have it and be in law enforcement."

"Psychics can't be cops? They are on TV."

"They can't be in real life, not if it's known. Police officers often have to testify in court. I would be discredited immediately because of what I can do. Some people think I'm a fraud. I've been called worse. I thought my father was wrong, but I've asked other officers I trust and I've even called other states. It's the same everywhere."

Rage burned through Charlie, hot and startling. It surprised him. Why was he so angry about someone verbally abusing Juliana? *Because no one had a right to hurt her.* Charlie choked down his rage and asked, "But it's something you want to do?"

"Yes. I want to follow in my father's footsteps. I want to be a detective."

Charlie felt speechless. Juliana had a dream she couldn't fulfill. In a perverse way, she was like him. Odd that he hadn't known about it. When she was younger she'd played cops and robbers with him but never mentioned her dream to him. Why not?

Then a thought struck him. "Did you always want to be one?"

Juliana looked away. "No. Only after my mom died."

Why then? He waited, but she didn't enlighten him. He probed a little. "That's when you became psychic."

She nodded. "I hit my head. Several holistic doctors told me that's sometimes how clairvoyance manifests."

He sensed the tension in her body. "I never knew."

"I didn't know what it was back then. I just knew something was different."

"So did I."

Juliana's smile flitted across her face. "That's not what I was talking about." But her stiff posture relaxed.

"Do you resent being psychic?"

"I resent being different, being treated differently or in a negative way. But I like being able to help the police." She drew in a deep breath. "How about I help you?" She laid her palm on the final photo. A sigh escaped her full lips. "It's here."

Excitement surged through Charlie. He scooted forward on the couch and looked at the web page address on the bottom of the paper. South Beach. Dalton Montgomery had it. "Can you tell me where the sculpture is in the house?"

Juliana closed her eyes and frowned. As seconds turned into minutes, she frowned harder. He could feel the tension in her. At last she opened her eyes. "I only get darkness."

"You mean you don't see anything?"

"No. I mean it's dark. Maybe it's inside something—a box, a drawer … "

"A safe?"

"I don't know. I couldn't tell."

"And you can't pinpoint better where it's at in the house?"

"Maybe if I was closer, or inside the house." She shrugged, the movement doing enticing things to her chest.

Charlie tore his eyes away from how the clingy white top lovingly cupped her breasts. "I don't know if I can get you in the house or not."

"I can't trespass, Charlie. My father's a cop."

"It's okay. I'm used to working on my own. Thanks for your help. You saved me hours, maybe days of stake-outs."

"You're welcome."

Charlie gathered his pictures into the manila file folder. He'd made it through this time with Juliana without making love to her. He'd better vamoose while both their good intentions were intact.

Juliana walked him to the door. He turned, his gaze sweeping from her tousled waves down to her glossy-painted toenails for what might be the last time. Her face hadn't changed; it was the same one that was branded on his heart. But her body had become a sexy, desirable one, one that he'd explored in the most intimate ways mere hours ago. One he wanted to explore again.

She studied him, too. Her eyes were soft with memories, perhaps the same ones playing in his mind.

Her full lips beckoned. What could it hurt to kiss her good-bye? He knew what, but he couldn't fight the urge to taste their succulent warmth one last time.

Charlie moved closer and leaned down to her. Juliana's eyes widened and her lips parted. He took possession of them. Desire surged up inside him. His arm stole around her bare waist and he pulled her to him, pressing her tight against his hungry flesh. He kissed her again and again, trying to assuage a need only she awoke. His erection was a burning brand between them.

Juliana's arms climbed his back. Her hips strained against his aching cock. She made needy sounds against his lips.

Need clawed at him. He turned with her and pressed her against her apartment wall. The file folder slid from his hand. Her thigh climbed his hip, opening her to him. He tore at his pants fly, snapping off the button in his haste. Juliana's hands interfered as he worked at getting his pants open. He gave way to her insistent fingers, instead reaching for the condom in his pocket. Had he known, suspected ... or hoped? Rational thought fled when she thrust her hand into his opened slacks and dived into his underwear to grip his cock. He groaned. It felt so good.

Charlie had enough brains left to push his pants and underwear down. Juliana helped him with the condom, although she nearly ended the encounter with her sensual handling. Then he slid his hands under that inviting skirt—did he have a thing about skirts?—up her smooth, firm thighs to her hips, and hit skin all the way.

"No panties," he panted.

Juliana lifted her leg in invitation. "They get in the way."

Charlie pressed his cock between her legs. "Too right." With one urgent thrust he filled her. They both groaned. Her pussy gripped him tight, her body's adjustments caressing his length.

God, it felt so good to be inside her again. But he had to move. He pressed her against the wall as he stroked into her tight body. He wanted to kiss her. He wanted to bare and suck her succulent breasts. But need overpowered all else, the need to fuse his body with hers.

He felt imminent orgasm and gritted his teeth to hold it back. He wasn't finished yet. It hadn't taken long enough. He gripped her bare butt, pulling her hard into his thrusts. But the urge was too strong, and when Juliana's internal spasms rhythmically milked his cock, he let go of his control. He swore he saw stars his orgasm was so powerful. His groan seemed to echo against the wall.

Charlie collapsed against her and moved his hands from her firm buttocks to wrap tight around her waist. Her heart pounded hard against his chest. Their breaths sawed in and out, slowing gradually.

He'd been fooling himself to think he could come here and not make love to her. And despite just having an orgasm, he wasn't done with her. He had to have her at least once more.

"I want to do that again slowly, very slowly. And I want it to take a very long time. And I want us to be naked. But first I want to kiss you and suck your breasts, and then I want to suck your clit."

Her pussy squeezed his still-erect cock. He shuddered.

"You have a lot of wants," she murmured in a husky voice.

"Yeah. Do you object?"

"No. I have some wants of my own."

"It might take awhile. Do you have the time?"

Juliana turned her head so she could look at him. "Do you? You're on an investigation."

Charlie gave her question serious deliberation. He had a lead he should pursue immediately. But buried to the hilt in Juliana's exquisite body he knew there was no place he'd rather be.

"I'm not done plumbing the depths of this lead." He thrust so she could feel he was serious about making love to her again.

"Umm," she hummed.

Charlie shuddered again, his body hungry to begin what he hoped would take hours. "We can use your uniform again. This skirt is nice, but there's something about a Catholic girl." He nuzzled her neck.

Juliana pushed his face away. "Charlie, I've grown up. Does the skirt represent the girl you knew back then?"

Charlie frowned. "No. I just think it's sexy. I think you're sexy now, too. I think you're sexy naked. I know you've grown up and I love the changes. I'd like to explore the changes if you'll let me."

She smiled and pulled him close for a kiss. But when he wanted the kiss to linger, she turned her head away. "I believe you said something about getting naked."

"Oh, yeah. We can play cops and robbers. You can be a suspect. It would involve frisking."

"Male officers can't frisk female suspects."

"I don't follow the rules. Especially when the suspect is as sexy as you."

"You may have to stay the night to interrogate me," she suggested. "I've got a lot to hide."

Charlie's smile felt like it split his face. "I believe this investigation is going to take all night. Perhaps a body cavity search is in order."

"Every nook and cranny," she agreed.

"Definitely. I have a long nightstick to probe those with." He thrust with his words.

She gasped. "You'll have to be ruthlessly thorough."

"Then I'll have to probe again and again." He put actions to words.

Her breath hitched. "Do whatever you have to do. I'll be interested to see your methods of interrogation."

CHAPTER 6

Charlie watched the sun rise over Dalton Montgomery's South Beach estate. Even at this early hour the estate showed activity. Through his binoculars he saw a delivery van arrive with the rental tables and chairs. A guard waved them through. Aha!

He waited five minutes after the truck disappeared into the estate, then drove up to the gate. With his brown contacts, black goatee, t-shirt and jeans, he looked like a young Latino.

The guard leaned down to the window. "State your business."

Charlie allowed an exaggerated Spanish accent to color his words. "I'm with Palisades Rentals but I missed the truck. I overslept, see, because I was with my honey last night. You know how it is, *amigo*." He didn't have to feign the effects of a night spent making love instead of sleeping. Two nights in a row. "I been chasing the truck since the warehouse, but the light turned red, see, and there was this cop at the intersection. Please, I'm in such trouble and I need this job."

"Follow the drive around the left to the pool house."

"*Gracias!*" Charlie drove through the gate. He kept his elation in check until he was driving past the manicured green lawn.

The house looked impressive as he approached. Two and a half stories of sprawling white surrounded the huge circular drive. The sheer number of windows should have presented him a daunting task of how many rooms he'd have to search for the sculpture. But he'd grown used to the mansions in Beverly Hills. Montgomery's house wouldn't thwart him.

Too soon he saw the split off to the pool house and took it. He parked away from the rental truck and approached it with a confident stride. He'd learned people assumed you belonged somewhere if you acted like you did.

Two men were pushing a cart full of white chairs down the ramp attached to the back of the truck.

"They told me to help," Charlie said. "I'm Chuck." He'd left his Latino accent at the gate.

The men looked at one another.

"You can push that cart." The bigger, brown-haired man gestured to another cart full of chairs off to the side. "Into the pool house. Danny's inside. Big guy, red hair. You can't miss him. He'll show you where to put it."

Charlie grunted acknowledgement and did as he'd been instructed. The pool house was bigger than his parent's three-bedroom home. The floors were shiny cream tile. The cart's rubber wheels made little sound as he pushed it down the short hallway to a room that looked like a small ballroom.

He spotted Danny immediately. "Big guy" had been an understatement. He was at least six-four with biceps as round as soccer balls.

Danny spotted him, too, and strode toward him. "Who are you?" It wasn't a casual question.

"Chuck. They told me to help you unload."

Danny's green eyes narrowed. "We're not going to steal anything."

Charlie shrugged. "I go where I'm told to go."

Danny's jaw muscles clenched. "Put that cart with the others. And for God's sake, don't run it into the columns."

Charlie bit back a smile. "Yes, sir."

Danny walked away cursing under his breath.

As Charlie went back and forth to the truck, he studied the layout of the house and grounds. There was the four-leaf clover pool Juliana had described. The property stretched to the ocean, where a small yacht was moored at the dock. He didn't know if that entrance to the estate was guarded like the front was, not that he planned to wait until nightfall to make an assault from the ocean. No, this wedding frenzy was the perfect cover to get in and out of the grounds. But he needed to get into the house. He was confident the sculpture wasn't in the pool house.

He watched for guards as he worked. He'd seen two more patrol the grounds. They could have been mistaken for businessmen in their lightweight suits, except for the slight bulges where they wore their guns and the cold look in their eyes. Charlie knew about guns. It had been part of his P.I. training. He knew how to fire one and practiced regularly with an actor friend, although he'd yet to purchase one of his own. He hadn't run into a situation where he'd needed to use one.

When the truck was emptied, Charlie wandered back to his car frustrated. He still hadn't gotten into the house. Boss man Danny ran a tight ship, and the few times he hadn't been close by, one of the guards had been patrolling. Charlie had listened to the Paradise Rentals workers, but hadn't learned much about the wedding. He needed details.

His shirt, the hair at his temples, and the back of his neck were damp with sweat. As he wiped his face and neck with a towel and gulped down water, another truck and a car full of Paradise Rental workers pulled in. Danny hadn't said anything about more chairs. In fact, he'd said they had five hundred, which to Charlie meant that was all of them. And they'd unloaded tables, too. What more could be coming?

He debated helping again as he stood under the relative shade of a palm tree, thankful for the ocean breeze, and sipped the remainder of his water. Other than the grounds layout, where the three sets of back doors were, and the guard patrols, he hadn't learned anything important in the forty-five minutes he'd been here. Unloading trucks wasn't his idea of a productive investigation.

One of the men he'd seen patrol by stopped as the driver pushed up the rollaway door of the truck. "That the tent?"

"Yep." The man didn't even stop to answer. The other men from the car stood waiting.

The guard turned and walked directly to the house.

Charlie straightened, all his senses on alert. Something was about to happen, and he needed to be in place when it did. He tossed the towel and empty bottle back in his car and sauntered to the truck. Again he gave them his story about being sent to help, and again they accepted him without question.

As they unloaded the heavy white tent, two people approached from the house, followed by the patrolling guard. Charlie tried not to stumble as he recognized Dalton Montgomery and his daughter, Haley, from the newspaper articles.

Dalton was a tall, well-groomed man with stylish brown hair. Haley was a slender twenty-two-year-old blonde who looked like she'd spent the night as Charlie had, and was irritated to be awakened at this hour. Her bee-stung lips told a story of recent use. Her red-and-white halter-top barely restrained her surgically enhanced breasts, and Charlie could see her erect nipples right through the fabric. Her skimpy red shorts should be illegal.

But he couldn't help comparing this ho look-alike to Juliana in ho drag. Juliana won in the sex appeal department hands down. Haley just looked like a spoiled brat.

Speaking of Juliana, Charlie wished she were here now to tell him what she could about Montgomery's involvement with the sculpture. He didn't look like a man who'd sent someone to steal it. Then again, he didn't look like someone entrenched in Miami's criminal underworld.

"My daughter will show you where she wants the tent," Montgomery said to the group.

"Yes sir, Mr. Montgomery," the driver replied.

The group of men took hold of the heavy tent and toted it past the pool onto a wide green lawn. The dew had dried under the hot Miami sun, which explained why the tent delivery had arrived later than the chairs.

"I want it here." Haley pointed to the ground at her feet.

The guard stepped forward and handed the driver a sheet of paper. "Here's the sprinkler layout so you can avoid puncturing the lines."

The driver nodded. "We've done this lots of times and no one's had a problem."

Charlie managed to get a spot close to Montgomery and his daughter as the Paradise workers began the arduous task of erecting the tent.

"The orchestra arrived last night," Montgomery told his daughter. "They're settled into the Hilton on the floor below the other guests."

Charlie noted the name of the hotel.

She huffed. "I hope they're not going to disturb the guests."

"I'm sure they won't."

Haley looked longingly toward the house. "I don't know why you had to get musicians from overseas."

"Only the best for you, Haley. It shows other people that we understand quality." Montgomery dropped his voice so Charlie had to strain to hear as he held onto the tent's rope, waiting his turn for the rope to be staked to the ground.

"And that outfit screams tramp. You're about to be married. I want you to look like a decent young woman."

She turned her angry face to him. "There's nothing wrong with what I'm wearing, Daddy. You're out of touch with fashion."

"I'm not out of touch. I want you to portray a little more chasteness as your wedding approaches. And to that end, I want you to move into a bedroom on the other side of the house ... alone."

"Daddy, that's ridiculous."

"It's not. It's only for one night. I don't want you looking like this on your wedding day."

Haley placed her hands on her hips. The pose thrust out her breasts and compromised the halter-top. Her lower lip jutted mulishly. "Like what?"

"Like you've just had sex."

Charlie turned away to bite back his laughter. He'd been right. He bet he'd looked like that when he arrived this morning. He wondered how Juliana looked. To his astonishment he began to grow erect picturing her the last time they'd made love … less than a handful of hours ago. Her lips, nipples, and the flesh between her legs had been flushed from overuse. But the satisfied look on her face had said she'd loved every minute of his handling. He'd hated leaving her.

"Careful, man," the Paradise worker next to him warned in a low voice. "You're gonna get fired if you keep thinking about that girl like that. She's the big boss's daughter, and this tent is for *her* wedding."

The man moved away before Charlie could correct him. But the reminder to keep his mind on business was an effective one. He was in the enemy camp, here to reconnoiter, not to reminisce.

A slender woman in a stylish linen pantsuit appeared from the direction of the house carrying a clipboard in her hands. She smiled when she saw the tent.

The workers staked down Charlie's line and he stepped back, giving him a clear view of the woman, Montgomery, and his daughter.

"I've double-checked where everything's to be placed, Mr. Montgomery. This wedding is going to go off without a hitch. The tent looks beautiful with the ocean backdrop."

"I chose the spot," the sulky Haley said.

"You chose well. The roses arrived safely. The florist is holding them in the cooler until tomorrow morning. Then they'll transport them here with the rest of the flowers and store them in the spare refrigerator in the main house. The cake was made yesterday. It's being flown out as we speak and will be stored in the caterer's cooler until a few hours before the wedding. Then it will be delivered here and stored in the pantry. The caterers will set it up during the wedding."

"I don't want deliveries getting in the way of guests arriving," Montgomery said. "Make them earlier if you have to."

"I know, Mr. Montgomery. They won't interfere. The out-of-town guests are settling into the Hilton. The hotel reports the Castletons cancelled due to an emergency."

The three of them moved away toward the house, but Charlie had gotten what he needed. He was called to help on the other side of the tent, but all he had to do was keep the rope taut while men drove stakes into the ground. His mind spun out scenarios. He could search the house if he came with the florist or the caterer. If he still couldn't find the sculpture, he could pretend to be this Castleton person.

Charlie didn't see a way into the house today. He might be able to sneak in tonight, but why risk it when there would be so many opportunities tomorrow?

When the tent was finished and the Palisades employees packed up, Charlie followed them out in his car. No sense lingering and drawing attention to himself. Despite not retrieving the sculpture, it had been a good day so far. He'd learned valuable information that could help him achieve his aim. He wondered how much better he could make it if he called Juliana.

CHAPTER 7

"That relic is going to be auctioned off tomorrow," Detective Montoya told Juliana. "Some guy named Dalton Montgomery is holding the sale."

Juliana held the phone between her cheek and shoulder as she straightened the typed pages of transcription. "If it's worth a drug route, why doesn't he keep it himself?"

"Montgomery's an up-and-coming player, but he has no rep with drugs that we can find. He may be doing it for the money. Drug dealers will pay plenty for that relic."

"Montgomery," Juliana mused. "I've heard that name recently."

"Probably because his only daughter's getting married tomorrow. It's been in all the society pages."

She frowned. "Didn't you say the auction is tomorrow?"

"Yeah. He must be using the wedding as a cover."

"That's cold." Juliana wondered again about the criminal mind.

"Yeah, but it gives us a chance to slip you in as a guest so you can find the relic."

"But I don't even know what it is."

"We're working on getting the information. But we need you at that wedding."

"I'm sure they'll ask for my invitation." She turned off her printer.

"Tell them you lost it."

Juliana snorted and paced her dining room along the sliding glass door. Idly she noted the plants on her deck needed watered. "At a society wedding nobody's going to believe that." Although if she was Charlie, she'd have no trouble lying her way inside.

"I'll see what kind of favor we can get from the press, maybe a press pass."

Juliana didn't want to know about that transaction. "What time is the wedding?"

"Two o'clock."

"I'll make sure I'm available in case you get what I need."

"Right." Montoya imbued that one word with a world of frustration before he hung up.

Juliana watered the poor plants. The dark pink Jacobinia, yellow coreopsis, orange milkweed, and pink periwinkles perked up instantly in their colorful homemade clay pots.

What did a spy wear to a society wedding? And how big was the house where she'd have to locate this relic? She did a web search and found stories about the wedding in all the Miami newspapers. There was plenty of information about Dalton Montgomery. And there was a photo of his mansion. Juliana let out her breath and leaned back in her chair.

She knew that house.

Her mind turned like tumblers clicking into place to open a safe. Charlie had gone to find a way into Montgomery's house to retrieve his client's sculpture, the relic worth a drug distribution pipeline.

Oh my God!

Charlie had no idea what he was getting into. He could be in danger right now. Her heart thumped against her rib cage. Her first instinct was to call him, but if he was sneaking around on Montgomery's property, she didn't want his phone to ring and jeopardize his safety.

She could call his brother, Rick. But tell him what? That his brother was trying to break into the house of a mobster wannabe to steal back a sculpture drug dealers would kill for? What would Rick do, stake out Montgomery's mansion? Haul his younger brother home by the scruff of the neck? Charlie was an adult, capable of playing any character and lying through his teeth. Maybe he wouldn't even get on the grounds. Surely Montgomery had the best security money could buy, including paid thugs to guard him.

Still, her heart continued to thunder.

Fine, she'd stop Charlie herself. She Mapquested the route to Montgomery's house, which said she could be there in thirty-five minutes. But what would she do when she got there? She knew Charlie had a dark gray rental car, but so did thousands of other Miamians. What if she couldn't find his car, or found it but not him? She wouldn't trespass on the grounds. What use was it for her to go there? He'd been gone for hours already. Anything could have happened during that time.

Juliana didn't want anything to happen to Charlie. If she ever had a chance to see him again she wanted him fully functional. She liked the way their two bodies combined seamlessly; four limbs entwined, four hands caressing, gripping, grasping, fondling, pressing.

Had her air conditioning failed? Juliana fanned herself. Her panties were damp. Again. She lifted the skirt of her little red sundress and fanned her crotch.

How could she get so hot so fast for a man she'd reconnected with only two days ago? No man had ever made her pant like a bitch in heat. She wanted him, and she wanted him *now*.

The doorbell rang, making her heart leap in her chest. *Charlie*. She ran to the door and checked the peephole—it was him! She hauled him inside her apartment with the intention of checking his functionality.

• • •

Charlie had a second to admire the short, sexy halter sundress Juliana wore before she plastered her lips to his. He was so pleased at her welcome he wrapped his arms around her waist and pulled her flush against him. As fast as her soft body touched his he had a hard-on. It was as though the past two nights with her had only whet his appetite.

She tugged at his jeans. He fumbled at the knot that secured the halter, and the material parted. He reached between them to palm her tight globes. Already her nipples were tight peaks.

"Fill me, Charlie," she begged, leaning into his caress. She had his jeans open and stroked his cock.

"I just got here," he complained half-heartedly. He wanted exactly what she wanted.

"I need you inside me." She found the condom in his pocket and sheathed him. Juliana tugged him into the living room where she wrestled with him, got her foot behind his leg and tumbled him backward onto the couch.

Then Juliana was all over him. She shoved her body down on his cock, her pussy gloving him tightly. Charlie arched with pleasure. She groaned, adjusting her body. And then she began to ride him, the little red skirt covering where they were joined. Her breasts bobbed as she moved, begging him. He pulled her down to suck the erect nipples. Juliana made little moans in the back of her throat. But soon she broke free to thrust almost desperately with him.

Charlie covered her breasts with his hands and thumbed the nipples. He loved her breasts. She let out a little shriek, and her internal contractions milked him. He gritted his teeth and held back his own orgasm, even though his hips bowed off the couch with his own thrusts.

Juliana was mad to mate, her face flushed with the passion she felt for him. He let her take him with near violence, slamming her body down on his cock until he swore he could go no deeper inside her.

Her living room echoed with the sound of flesh slapping against flesh, tortured breaths, and groans of near pain. But it couldn't go on. He was fighting for control, fighting to make love for as long as they could. But it was too hot, too primal.

He reached between them to stroke his fingers across her clit. Juliana shrieked and arched, her body squeezing his. Charlie rocketed over the edge into free fall. His heels pressed into the couch so that his butt didn't even touch the fabric.

Juliana collapsed onto him, kissing his neck. He wrapped his arms around her and relaxed his body against the couch.

After catching his breath, he said, "That was some welcome."

"You could have been killed!"

"If that was your intention, you nearly succeeded."

Juliana lifted her head from his chest. "I meant going to Dalton Montgomery's house. Did you get the sculpture?"

"Not yet, but I'm going to try again tomorrow."

She gripped his arms. "He won't let that sculpture go without a fight. He's auctioning it tomorrow to a bunch of drug dealers. It's worth billions in illegal drugs."

"I know."

CHAPTER 8

"You knew the sculpture was worth billions and yet you went there anyway?" Juliana exclaimed, her brown eyes wide with shock.

"My client has very personal and compelling reasons for wanting that sculpture back," Charlie explained.

"Well, he can't have it. Miami narcotics detectives have to get it off the street. Allowing more drugs into the city is unthinkable."

Charlie narrowed his eyes. "But it's not their sculpture. It belongs to my client, and that's where I'm going to return it."

"Charlie, you can't go back to Montgomery's house. It's too dangerous. I told you about the drug dealers so you'd understand why you have to stay away."

"The wedding preparations are the perfect way to gain entrance to the grounds. I was there all morning blending in with the help. I'll be fine."

Juliana sat up, which drove his cock deeper into her. She shuddered with pleasure, which did exciting things to her bare breasts. Charlie still had a hard-on, despite the topic.

"It's a needless risk," she said. "I've already talked to the detectives, and they're going to get me into the wedding. Now that I know what the sculpture looks like, I can probably find it easily."

"My way is less risky." He narrowed his eyes. She wanted *his* sculpture.

"Tell me what it is and I'll notify the cops."

"No way I'm giving away that information."

Juliana captured his wrists on either side of his head. "Charlie, this isn't a game, and it's no place for an amateur sleuth. This is police business."

The woman he was making love to didn't believe in his capability. Boy, how deflating. This was why he hadn't told his family what he'd done with his life. Those who'd known him when he was younger didn't believe he could change. They didn't believe he was capable of holding a serious job. He'd always be the clown, goofing off, and playing make-believe. Billy would always be considered the smart one. The serious one. The worthwhile one.

Charlie tried to let Juliana's doubt roll off him. All that mattered was that he prove to *himself* that he'd made something meaningful of his life. But, damn it, he wanted Juliana to think so, too. Once, she'd thought the world of him.

Gently, he pushed her to the side, scooted to the edge of the couch, and stood up.

"Charlie?"

"I should go." He strode into the bathroom to dispose of the condom and wash up.

He sensed her behind him. He didn't look up, but continued to wash his hands.

"Charlie."

Her slender hand stopped him as he reached for the towel and turned him to face her. She stood there in her glorious nudity. The hard-on that had been fading rose once more.

Her brown eyes were filled with concern and confusion. "What did I say?"

"It doesn't matter."

"It does."

Charlie noted she kept hold of his wrist. What did she sense with her psychic ability when she touched him? Did she sense the lost boy who'd found a path to take him out of the mire of grief over Billy's death?

Charlie tried to explain. "I've been a P.I. for two years. Nothing else. All I have is my reputation. If I go back to California empty-handed, my client won't refer me to anyone else, and he'll never use my services again. Word will get around that I don't deliver. Jobs will dry up. It's hard enough starting out as a P.I. I don't need any more strikes against me."

Her mouth opened and closed several times without saying anything. She was a cop's daughter—her loyalty was to them. And he knew it was hard for her to accept what he said. He sighed. Subconsciously he'd hoped to spend another night with her. He'd just had her—or she him—yet he wanted her again and knew he'd want her a time or two after that.

But was she making love to him, or to a memory?

"I don't understand you," she said.

"I know." He gathered her nude body against him. The scent of sex was strong on her. It hardened his erection even further. She felt so good against him. Even though he knew he should kiss her goodbye and leave, his hands roamed her back down to her firm buttocks. She hummed her pleasure.

Maybe just once more, for the last time.

She got a condom on him before they sank to the floor. It was a tight fit in the bathroom. A little gymnastic contortion and then it was an even tighter fit inside her body. Then he was giving it—and her—his all, letting them both know the pleasure they'd be missing, how good it was between them.

His ears rang with his exertions.

"Was that the doorbell?" she gasped.

He didn't care. They'd just got their rhythm synchronized and found movements that didn't bang his head or shoulders into anything. He wasn't giving this up for the next hour if he was lucky.

But whoever was at the door wasn't giving up either. The person rang the bell over and over. It was damn distracting.

"Charlie, let me up."

"No, damn it. Whoever it is can wait."

But apparently they couldn't. Charlie heard the front door open. Somebody had a key. Crap! He bashed his head on the sink and saw stars. "Ow!"

"Oh no!" Juliana wriggled out from under him and grabbed a bath towel just as a bellow preceded Captain Sanchez himself, catching them in the act for the second time in fifteen years.

"Oh, shit!" three people swore.

CHAPTER 9

Juliana's father waited in the kitchen while they dressed. Neither she nor Charlie had had an orgasm, so he had to be as frustrated as she was. She noted he was semi-erect. Her lower body burned with what they hadn't finished. But her father's entrance prevented further sexcapades.

"I'm sorry," she said.

He shrugged, smiling. "I should be used to it by now." He leaned down to give her a warm kiss. When he was finished, she felt warm all over. "This time would have been great."

"Yeah. Are you ready to face my father?"

"No, but I won't let you take the heat alone."

His comment made her chest feel tight. She led him out to the kitchen where her father sat, his face devoid of expression. His gaze scanned her first, then zeroed in on Charlie.

"Charlie Ziffkin."

"Captain Sanchez." Charlie moved closer to her to face her father.

Her father's eyes narrowed, and he frowned at Charlie's neck. Then Juliana remembered the love bite. She groaned silently.

"I won't ask what's going on. That's obvious," her father said. "And it's obvious it's not the first time."

Juliana blushed over the reminder of her hickey the other day. "We're adults, Papá. We're not doing anything wrong."

"And what have you got to say, Ziffkin?"

"Juliana is helping me with a case."

Her father's brown eyes narrowed. "Helping you how?"

"You know how, Papá. He's trying to retrieve a stolen sculpture for a client."

"Why aren't the police involved?" her father echoed her question from yesterday.

"Sir, you know sometimes private detectives can go where cops can't. This is one of those times," Charlie explained.

Juliana jerked. He'd tossed out that plausible lie without hesitation.

"So this stolen item is the reason you were arrested for solicitation?" Her father gave her a pointed look.

"Yes, sir. A misunderstanding. I get that a lot."

"And then you came here to Juliana's apartment."

Charlie glanced at her. She tried to signal with her eyes to evade.

"Do you have a problem with me being here, Captain Sanchez?" Charlie asked.

"Why don't we step outside," her father suggested.

"Dad, don't be medieval."

"Mr. Ziffkin, would you step outside please." It was his fearsome cop voice. Even Juliana's stomach quailed.

But she rallied. "You're not in charge of my life, Dad. I think you'd better leave."

"It's okay, Juliana," Charlie said. "I have to go anyway."

Before she could protest, he leaned down to kiss her. She knew her father was watching, but when Charlie wrapped his arm around her waist and pulled her against him, she was only aware of the desire that surged between them. His hard erection pressed into her belly. Why couldn't he just let her father leave so they could spend the rest of the day in bed together?

Too soon the kiss ended. Charlie's blue eyes were sad. But then he smiled like a rogue.

"You could come back," she whispered. "We could finish what we started."

"I can't. I have an appointment."

She didn't believe him.

Charlie released her. Her father's face was as stony as she'd ever seen it. The two men stepped out the door to discuss her. Why couldn't her father accept that she was grown and could take care of herself?

• • •

As soon as they were out of earshot of her apartment, Juliana's father asked, "What are your intentions toward Juliana?"

Charlie answered honestly. "I'm returning to California as soon as I retrieve the stolen item."

"Juliana's not a one-night stand."

"I never thought she was."

"Juliana's in awe of you, a movie star—"

"I'm not a movie star. And Juliana doesn't think of me like that. If anything, I'm still seventeen-year-old Charlie to her, only in an adult body."

Captain Sanchez narrowed his eyes. "You're saying her sleeping with you is taking up where you left off all those years ago?"

"Yes, sir. And for me, too." The realization was like a bright light shining in the stygian darkness. His body had grown up, lived years away from her, but it was like an alternate universe. The moment he'd finished what they started all those years ago, the clock in this reality began to tick again.

"I did what was best back then," her father said. "I didn't want her unwed and pregnant."

"That wouldn't have happened," Charlie insisted. "My dad taught me about birth control. We would have been careful."

"Accidents happen."

"Then she could have lived at my house. My mom would have taken care of her and the baby."

"So I'd lose my daughter just after losing her mother!" Captain Sanchez looked shocked, and then his face wiped clean of expression.

"You didn't have to send Juliana away, somewhere you thought she'd be safe from me, while you packed up the house," Charlie accused. "It wasn't right for her. Or me."

"You were planning to move to Hollywood when you graduated. You would have broken her heart soon enough."

"She could have come with me." Should have been with him. Her presence might have made him decide to make a career change sooner. Maybe he'd have moved back home. Maybe then Billy wouldn't have gone to New Orleans. Then he'd be alive now. And so would Charlie.

Her father had held onto Juliana, afraid to lose her. If Charlie had more time, he'd break her out of her prison.

To do what? Share his cell?

Charlie glanced back at Juliana's apartment. Then he looked at Captain Sanchez. "It was wrong to take her away from me." He strode to his car. He had to clear out of his hotel room and relocate to the Hilton.

As he drove away, he saw that Captain Sanchez still stood where Charlie had left him. His frown was thoughtful.

But Charlie's plans for a quick getaway from his hotel were thwarted when he found Rick sitting in a chair in his room. Charlie's stomach twisted in knots.

"I won't ask how you got in."

"You haven't called Mom and Dad," Rick said.

"I'm working. I told you that already."

"24/7?"

"You should understand that." Charlie flopped down on the bed.

"You're not working now."

"Yes I am. I came back to get some clothes." All of them actually.

"Then where are you going?"

"I have to establish my identity for this case. I have to set up."

"Like you're working undercover?"

"Yeah."

"Like acting?"

"Yeah."

He could see the wheels turning in Rick's mind. "Need help?"

"No." Then Charlie tacked on, "Thanks."

Rick considered that for a few moments. "You haven't returned any of my messages. I've called here repeatedly and you never answer, even at night."

"I told you—"

"One of the vice cops said you left with Juliana Sanchez the other night." Rick had given him that look many times before.

Two inquisitions in thirty minutes. Was he thirty or thirteen? "I followed her out. It was good to see her again. We talked."

"Talked." Rick repeated, although the spin he put on the word was exactly the type of activity Charlie and Juliana had engaged in. "You've got a hickey on your neck."

Charlie wasn't about to kiss and tell, not about Juliana.

When he said nothing, Rick added, "Her dad's a captain now."

"I know." Charlie smiled at his brother, charm to charm. Rick had mastered charm as a police officer, but Charlie had been born with it.

"He's got a whole squad to beat your ass now if he catches you with his daughter."

Charlie snorted. "Cops have to follow the rules. I learned that at P.I. school."

"Correspondence course?"

The jab hurt, but Charlie shrugged it off. "Sure. I can't wait to take my handguns course."

That wiped Rick's face clear of expression. "That's not funny, Charlie."

"Sorry, I thought it was. I need to get moving." Charlie climbed off the bed.

Rick rose, too. "Can't it wait an hour? Mom and Dad want to see you."

"There's some urgency to this case. The sooner I get into place, the sooner it's solved."

"You used to be more flexible."

He used to be many things. "I'm grown up now, just like you; I have responsibilities."

Charlie could see the doubt in Rick's frown. He had to get that sculpture back so he could return to California before his parents sought him out themselves. In California at least some people thought him adult and capable.

Rick pulled out his wallet, and for a moment Charlie flinched, expecting an offer of money. But Rick slid a business card from it, wrote a number on the back, and held it out to Charlie.

"Here's my cell and Mom and Dad's phone number."

Charlie didn't take it. "I know their number."

"Coulda fooled me." Rick dropped the card onto the dresser. "Call them."

Rick left, and Charlie sagged with relief. His muscles ached from the tension he'd felt being in the same room with his brother. His family expected the same old Charlie, but that young man had died with Billy.

His mind was made up. He packed his things and took them to the car. As soon as it got dark tonight he would make a night raid on Montgomery's house. If that didn't work, he'd already be set up at the Hilton for his contingency plan to get into the house with the wedding guests. And he still had two more tries tomorrow before the wedding with the florist and the caterer. But the sooner he got the sculpture, the better.

He could do this without Juliana; after all, he'd been doing it for two years without her. But he wished she were helping him this time.

CHAPTER 10

"He's still the same Charlie Ziffkin." Juliana's father faced her across her little wooden kitchen table. He stood with his hands on his hips while she sat toying with a Diet Pepsi. "He's going back to California."

"I know that."

"Then why would you let him sleep with you?"

"Because I wanted to." She sighed. "Listen, Dad, I know you won't understand, but I wanted to know what it would have been like if you hadn't stopped us. And I'm glad I did."

"You aren't falling for him, are you?"

"No." She'd done that long ago, when she and Charlie were teenagers, when things had changed. *She'd* changed; so had Charlie. His voice had begun to deepen, he'd grown taller, and she'd felt attracted to him as she'd never been before. She'd begun to have trouble breathing when she shared a room with him. She'd dreamt about kissing him, wondering what his lips would feel like.

"That's good," her father said, breaking into her sad reverie, "because nothing could come of it."

"What would have happened if Mamá hadn't died?" Juliana asked. "Would you have packed me off to Tía Dolores's house if Mamá had been alive?"

"Your mamá would have been able to talk to you about boys and ... well ... sex." His tanned cheeks grew ruddy.

"*You* could have talked to me about it."

"These things need a mother's touch."

"Yet you'll tell the boys the facts of life."

"Your brothers are boys, Juliana. Of course a man will discuss that with them."

She sighed, rose and moved to his side. "Papá, I'm no different than Emilio and Juan. We're all your children. You don't need to treat me like I'm glass."

"I'm treating you with respect, as a man should."

She ignored the accusation in the last part of his statement. "You're treating me like I'm incapable, which I'm not."

"*M'hija*, we've gone over and over this. You're always going to be my little *chica*."

Yes. Frozen at sixteen when her mother died. She walked him to the door.

He cleared his throat. "Were you able to help Narcotics?"

"No." Juliana told him what they wanted and why. But she held back from telling him she could find the object. Not only was Charlie linked to it, but she hoped to surprise him by retrieving the sculpture first. If the narcs could get her into the wedding, she'd see if a memory of the picture worked as well as a photo.

"That's a shame," her father said. "I'd hate to see more drugs in this town. It's hard enough to win the fight against them."

Juliana kissed him on the cheek. "Give my love to my step-mamá."

"I will. You could come for dinner this weekend."

"Maybe Sunday. I'll let you know."

After he left, Juliana felt too antsy to type medical transcriptions. Usually the familiar words and phrases and surgeon's voices had a soothing rhythm. And sounds carried no psychic connections. But right now she didn't want to hear about heart bypass and angioplasty procedures. In her spare bedroom she donned a man's large t-shirt over her clothes. She dug out a large wad of moist clay from a fifty-pound box and set it in the center of her potter's wheel, sliding onto the round stool. She started the wheel spinning with the foot pedal. The clay was cool to the touch. As usual, she felt nothing when she touched it. It had no associative emotions or memories.

This was going to be a red pot. She'd seen a photo of a red Mexican pot with orange, yellow, and green peppers on it. She liked to visualize the pot in her mind as she formed it. Her hands smoothed the clay into a circle as the wheel turned. Her palms slid across the cool, moist clay. She formed the mouth of it by pressing her fingers into the center. With gentle pressure, she widened the orifice.

Charlie had done this to her last night, spreading her pussy open until he could push his tongue inside. Her body tightened in memory. The sensation had been exquisite, especially when he rubbed her clit at the same time. She'd come screaming. Twice. Finally her pleading had forced him to cease his torment and fill her with his cock.

The pot's opening was now wide enough to slip her hand inside. The moldable clay gave outward under her gentle pressure, the way Charlie had spread her legs before he feasted on the tender flesh there, his dark head bent between her tanned thighs. She relived the feeling of his tongue caressing and probing, laving her quivering, excited flesh, pushing her with insistent jabs toward that explosion they both desired.

She was using too much pressure on the clay and eased up. Charlie did this when he wanted to extend their loving. He left her trembling while he paid tribute to other parts of her body, only to return to excite the flesh between her legs once more. Sometimes when they were on the brink, he slowed his thrusts until he barely moved. Then he would kiss her until they were gasping for breath. Slowly he'd build the speed again.

Two nights they'd been together, and it hadn't been enough. She ached for his possession, ached to be molded and caressed, pressed into, filled with warm, hard flesh. She was an empty vessel, just like this pot. She'd been empty since she'd been ripped from Charlie's arms all those years ago. Only he could make her feel completely alive.

But she'd never see him again if she gave the relic to the detectives.

It was laughable. She'd found what she'd lost, only she couldn't keep it. Hadn't she learned that the hard way when her mother died? People left you. There was nothing you could do to stop it.

But she wished she could have more time with him.

• • •

Charlie strode confidently into the Hilton with his luggage. This was going to be a little tricky, but he was determined to succeed.

"May I help you, sir?" The young blonde woman's nametag read Natalie.

"I hope so. The name's Castleton. My wife and I had a reservation with the Montgomery wedding party but we canceled when we didn't think we'd be able to make it. Things worked out, and my wife insisted we come. Please tell me you have a room available?" Charlie gave his most charming smile.

"Let me check, Mr. Castleton." Her French manicured fingertips tapped on the keys. Then a smile broke out on her face. "You're in luck. Your original room is still available. You'll be on the same floor with the other wedding quests."

"Excellent," Charlie said. "And you've got all our information in your computer?"

"Yes. Joseph and Camille Castleton." She rattled off their address and phone number in Atlanta, and Charlie confirmed it.

"That's for two nights," Natalie said.

Charlie kissed part of his finder's fee good-bye. He'd have to get a credit card advance and pay the bill in cash. "Yes."

"Ah," Natalie murmured, her finger on the screen.

Charlie tensed, awaiting discovery.

"The Montgomerys are paying for their guests to stay." She smiled at Charlie. "There won't be a bill for you to worry about."

Charlie exhaled and smiled back at her. "The Montgomerys are good people."

He finished registering, pocketed both key cards, and allowed a bellhop to escort his luggage to his room. The king-sized bed called out for him to sink his tired body into its thick mattress. Fatigue pulled at him after two nights with little sleep. But he was used to odd sleep schedules when he filmed movies.

He tipped the bellhop and laid out black jeans, a black T-shirt, and his suit jacket. A quick shower washed away Juliana's scent, which he immediately regretted. But their affair was finished unless he stopped at her house one last time on his way out of town.

Charlie eyed the big bed. It would be a perfect place for a sexual romp with Juliana. He sat on the side. It felt wonderfully soft. They wouldn't have to worry about waking the neighbors with their gymnastics because the mattress would absorb even the roughest play and no one would get hurt.

With a sigh, he lay down. Alone. He and Juliana hadn't finished in the bathroom when her father interrupted, which was why he ached for her now. He set his watch alarm for eleven o'clock. He'd snatch some sleep, then grab something to eat, and hopefully sneak into the Montgomery mansion while darkness hid him.

Damn, he wished Juliana were here to hold in his arms.

•••

Through his small binoculars, Charlie saw quite a few lights on in the Montgomery mansion even though it was past midnight. He'd snuck through the yard of the unlit house next door, then down to the dock so he could approach from the back of the house. Thank God there wasn't a moon tonight, but to be safe, his fake beard and mustache covered much of the paler skin on his face.

He'd only seen one guard patrolling, and that was fifteen minutes ago. Time to move. He rose from the shadowed side of the guesthouse and strolled toward the back door of the main house. Fifteen yards had never seemed so far. Despite his caution, he felt incredibly alive.

He tried the doorknob and found it locked. The four-season porch was to his left, a much more visible target, but he had to try it. He inhaled and strode onto the patio. Five sets of doors opened outward. Feeling conspicuous, he tried the first one. It was locked. So was the second. The third turned under his hand.

Taking a deep breath, Charlie opened it far enough to slip through, then pulled it closed behind him. No sense drawing attention to his point of entry. Faint light from the hall illuminated the chairs, couches, and tables on this indoor patio. He avoided the obstacles and flattened himself next to the doorway, cursing for not researching the floor plan as he usually would. Instead, he'd been making love to Juliana.

Charlie blocked that thought before it could proceed further. He couldn't afford any distractions. The front door was ahead of him to the right, but would Montgomery's study be to the left or the right? The house was taller on his right, which meant stairways leading to bedrooms. He turned left.

His black running shoes made no sound on the polished tile floor. The hall opened into a gleaming kitchen, the stainless steel appliances reflecting the lone light in the room. Charlie turned into the hallway on his right. The floor here was highly polished wood. Someone's footstep alerted him and he immediately backtracked, ducking into the spacious kitchen. As he flattened against the wall, he looked for cover and another way out. His heart was hammering so loud he could barely hear the approaching footsteps. Male, by the sound of the heavier tread. Definitely not high heels.

Locating another door, he prepared to fling himself in that direction. As he stood poised, the footsteps continued on, the sound more muffled on the tile. He let out his breath.

Charlie waited a beat, then swung back out into the hall. With extreme caution he padded forward and checked the first doorway. It was a formal dining room with a large table and what looked like twenty chairs. Then came a formal pantry, a lounge, and then, bingo … a room with a desk and a computer.

There was only one doorway and he was standing in it. A wall of windows behind the desk showed the paved front courtyard. Damn. He'd have to use a penlight to search the dim room, which someone patrolling the grounds could see through the windows.

There was no hope for it. Without Juliana to pinpoint the sculpture's location, he had to search methodically. There were two paintings on the wall. He lifted the one closest to the door, looking for a wall safe. The hall light showed nothing behind it. The next painting hung on the wall by the desk. Using his body to block the small light, he flashed his penlight behind the painting. It, too, was bare.

Keeping his thumb over the majority of the light, he swept the top of the credenza. Not that he'd expected the sculpture to be out in the open after what Juliana had said. The credenza was locked. He used his lock picks to open it, but there were only file folders inside. Charlie didn't know enough about Montgomery to understand what was in the files. Besides, he was here for the sculpture.

He checked the desk next, picking it open with his tools. There was a built-in safe in the bottom drawer big enough to hold the relic. Charlie's heart raced as he inserted his pick in the lock. He fumbled the first try. Then he inhaled and breathed out to calm himself. The lock clicked, a sound like a gunshot in the room's silence.

Charlie lifted the lid … and heard a second click and the sound of leather soles on wood. He dropped to the plush carpet. The footsteps halted. A beam of light splayed over the desktop. He didn't dare breathe. The light clicked off and the footsteps moved on.

He rose and shone the penlight into the safe. It contained several bundles of money, hundred dollar bills, some papers—titles and deeds—several small notebooks filled with mostly numerical data, several flash drives, and more papers. But no sculpture. He clenched his fist in frustration. It should be here. He replaced everything and searched the rest of the desk, the closet, and the room. Nothing. Dammit. Montgomery must have it in a bedroom safe. Charlie couldn't risk a search of the bedrooms at this hour. He'd have to try again in the morning.

Charlie slipped his tools and penlight into his pocket. Then he flattened against the door and listened. When he heard nothing, he slipped into the hallway and headed toward the back of the house.

Would Montgomery move the sculpture downstairs before the wedding? It would be easier to produce the sculpture for potential bidders if he did. Charlie would search the office again in the morning.

Another sound alerted him just in time and he darted into the pantry, flattening himself against the wall. Footsteps stopped. Charlie held his breath and stilled his body.

They both seemed to stand frozen, listening. Charlie hadn't thought he'd made a sound coming down the hall, but he'd been a little distracted. He cursed his stupidity. He had to stay focused in the present. And the present was right outside the door.

The need to breathe was immediate. He'd learned to play dead for some of his roles where the rise and fall of a corpse's chest could force the filmmaker to reshoot a scene. He let out a slow, careful breath and took in air. There was a rustle of cloth, and Charlie froze again. Then there was a footstep and another and another as the guard proceeded down the wooden hall.

That had been too close. It was time to leave. He listened for a minute and then poked his head into the hall to look both ways. Seeing no one, he stepped into the hall and as quickly and silently as he could, retraced his steps to the indoor patio. A scan of the back lawn showed him the coast was clear, so he strode out to the guesthouse.

It had been both harder and easier than he'd thought.

"Hey!" a man shouted behind him.

Charlie flung himself toward the palm trees. A gunshot rang out. A hot pain seared his left bicep. He bit back a curse, dropped, and rolled, coming up against a palm tree. Another shot caused bark chips to spray from the tree trunk next to him.

Crap, the guy was trying to kill him! Charlie switched direction, diving for the bushy Florida Gama grass. But he kept on scrambling backward. The grass wouldn't stop a bullet.

The hedge separating the Montgomery's property from the absent neighbor's was four feet wide. Charlie launched himself over it, rolled to his feet, and took off running. Any second he expected a bullet to pierce his back. How ironic that he'd come home to die.

His lungs burned. This was stupid. Running would attract attention to him. He should hide. But he'd never been shot at, never had someone try to kill him before. He couldn't stand still and let someone murder him.

Like someone had murdered Billy. Stabbed him in the back.

Shit! Charlie ran faster. Should he head straight for his car three doors down? Would they catch him then? The twelve-foot-high hedge that separated the houses protected him now, unless the guard was following him. Charlie couldn't hear any pursuit. Did they have radios? God, what had he been thinking to come here at night?

He'd have to risk his car. It was his fastest getaway. He pounded down the driveway to the gate. A latent sense of self-preservation halted him there. A runner would bring unwonted attention on the street. But someone strolling to his car wouldn't.

His nerves screamed to move faster, but he forced himself to walk toward his car. He was exposed. They'd be looking for him. He was moving too slow. Why had he parked so far away?

Sweat ran down the sides of his face into his fake beard. His T-shirt stuck to his chest and back. The hair on his neck clung with dampness.

God, let me make it to my car. His back itched. Was a gun trained on him even now? Would he be brought down like a rabid dog? Would anyone even care if he was? His parents, his brothers. But would they care as much about him as they had about Billy?

Charlie now regretted every year he'd been forced to spend away from Juliana. If he thought he'd wasted his life as an actor, it was an even bigger waste without the one woman who seemed the other half of him. She was yin to his yang. Dammit, why had he left her this afternoon like that?

He drew his car keys from his pants pocket. The lights would flash if he clicked the door open, so he'd have to do it the old-fashioned way. His internal clock screamed that he was running out of time. With shaking hands, he inserted the key, unlocked the car, and opened the door. The light bloomed like a beacon in the night. But no one slammed the door shut. He slid behind the wheel. No one leaped from the bushes to point a gun in his face. When he reached out to shut the door his arm screamed in pain. He looked in surprise at the trail of red sliding down his arm toward his wrist.

No time. Don't think about it now. He had to get that light off. He closed the door and locked it. Darkness reigned. His hand shook as he stuck the key in the ignition. The car faced away from Montgomery's mansion. He felt his back exposed. He saw a dark figure appear on the street. Charlie started the car without putting his foot on the brake. The car lurched forward. He left the headlights off and accelerated slowly.

Too slowly. They had cars. It was miles to the freeway. He drove as fast as he dared, watching for headlights in his rearview mirror. When he passed a house lit up with a line of cars parked at the curb, he pulled into a vacant spot and turned off the engine. His mind screamed at him to run, but someone had seen him pull away. They'd catch up to him and then … He was safer here for now.

In a moment, headlights appeared in his side mirror. Charlie slid down in his seat. Two cars roared past. His heart thumped hard. That had been close.

While he waited to see if more cars pursued, he pulled out his ponytail and stripped off the false beard and mustache. He used his teeth to tie a bandana around his arm.

Still he waited. Ten minutes later, headlights appeared from the opposite direction and he ducked out of sight. Two cars passed at an unhurried pace. He stayed down out of sight for five more endless minutes. His arm throbbed to his heartbeat.

Then he sat up and started the car. Still without turning on his headlights, he drove a mile down the road. When he didn't see any pursuit behind him, he switched on his lights.

Charlie didn't breathe easy until he reached the freeway. Even then he took an exit going the opposite direction from where he wanted to go, drove around in circles until he was sure he hadn't been followed, and then drove back to the freeway.

He felt a little lightheaded with relief. Still, he headed to the one place that felt like home.

To Juliana.

CHAPTER 11

Charlie nearly fell through her doorway when Juliana opened the door to his pounding.

"Hush, you'll wake the neighbors. Do you know what time it is?" she whispered.

"Hammer time?" He gave her a silly, lopsided smile.

"Are you drunk?"

"Do I seem drunk?"

"I asked, didn't I?" Juliana didn't smell liquor. "Are you high?"

"High on life, baby." He took a step forward and lurched toward her.

"You *are* high." She closed the door, sighing. When she'd seen him she'd felt a thrill go through her because she'd thought he'd come to make love.

"No." He shook his head and thrust a bandana-wrapped arm out to her. "Wounded."

"Wounded?" It came out a small shriek. Then she remembered who she was talking to—the actor. "How?"

"Gunshot." He looked smug.

She sucked in her breath. "Let me see."

"Can I sit down first?"

He was paler than when she'd seen him earlier. What if he was telling the truth? Juliana led him to her small kitchen and turned on the bright overhead light. He sat in a chair with an audible sigh and wiped sweat from his forehead.

She untied the navy bandana. There was a dark stain on it. It clung to his arm and he hissed. She peeled it loose. There was a round hole near the edge of his bicep.

"You've been shot!"

"Told you so."

"Someone shot you." Juliana couldn't believe it. She turned his arm looking for an exit wound. There. Another round hole. She breathed a sigh of relief. It was bad enough but at least a doctor wouldn't have to dig out the bullet.

"We have to get you to the hospital."

"No." His jaw set mulishly.

She nodded at his arm. "This could get infected."

"Pour some alcohol or peroxide on it."

"That isn't funny, Charlie. This is serious. I have to report it."

Charlie grabbed her hand with his uninjured one. "Do that and you sign my death warrant."

"What are you talking about?"

"You don't think Montgomery's men will be watching all the hospitals to see if anybody matching my general description comes in with a gunshot wound? How long after that do you think I'd live?"

Juliana had never seen him this serious. She frowned. The laughing man who'd barged in her apartment was a far cry from the man sitting in her kitchen now.

"This might need stitches. I'm no doctor."

"Just clean and disinfect it and bandage it for now. And give me some aspirin. I need to function for another twenty-four hours. Can you do that for me?"

His brown eyes—brown?—pleaded with her. Why had he come to her instead of going to his family?

"You could call your brother. Rick's a policeman. He can help. He can protect you."

"I don't want his protection. I take care of myself."

"You didn't do so well tonight. You want to tell me how this happened?"

He sighed. "Peroxide and aspirin first."

Juliana collected what she'd need. When she returned to the kitchen, Charlie had removed his black T-shirt. Her heart sped up at the sight of his firm chest … until she saw the drop of blood sliding down his arm.

"Hold that over the sink." She dropped her items on the counter.

Reaching into the cupboard above the stove, she located a bottle of Jose Cuervo. She poured a full shot and dumped two aspirins in her hand. She held them out to Charlie, who now stood at the sink.

"Cuervo. You don't mess around." His eyes were blue once more. He downed the pills and the contents of the shot glass in one gulp then coughed. "Damn good stuff."

"Need more?"

"I'm good for the moment."

"In the movies they pour booze onto the wound," she said.

"They use whiskey in the movies."

She held up the bottle to read the label. "This has got a pretty high alcohol content."

"That'd be wasting good liquor. Use the cheap stuff." He nodded toward the bottles of rubbing alcohol and peroxide.

"You want a bullet to bite down on?" she asked.

"No gun. And this one went all the way through."

"I could call my dad. He could help you."

Charlie shook his head. "He'd want to know why I came to you."

Juliana cocked her head. "Why did you?"

"It was the only place I could think of."

She thought he was only telling part of the truth. "It's late. If you're going to scream when I pour peroxide on your arm I'd prefer you bite on a towel or something."

Charlie clutched his chest. "You wound me, and I'm already wounded. You call my manhood into question …"

They both looked at his crotch. Juliana frowned. He didn't have a hard-on.

"Well, that's a disappointment," Charlie said to his groin. Then he lifted his head and gave her a sheepish look. "Anyway, men don't scream—"

"*You* might."

"They yell," he overrode her words.

"I think you need a gag."

"I want to present the correct manly impression here."

"Don't worry about that. After the last few nights, I couldn't possibly think you're not a man."

Charlie's smile was downright smug. "In that case, I'll take a towel."

She held his arm over the sink and poured alcohol on the wounds. Charlie jerked and his yell was muffled in the towel. She hated hurting him. Then she pressed the peroxide into both wounds. When he set the towel aside, he was breathing hard, his head hanging. She poured him another shot of Cuervo and wrapped his shaking fingers around it. He tossed it back in one gulp.

"You're trying to get me drunk so you can have your way with me," he said.

"Charlie, you're so easy all I have to do is look at you and you get a hard-on."

"Only with you."

She wished that were true. "I'll do the best I can with these bandages, but I'll have to go to the store and buy bigger ones."

"Okay."

"What, no argument?" She stuck big Band-Aids over the holes.

He winced. "No energy at the moment. I'm gonna need to lie down."

"Almost done." She grabbed an Ace bandage from the table. His brown contacts were in a little contact case. That reminded her he still hadn't told her why he'd been at Montgomery's house in disguise although she feared she knew. Later. Right now she had to finish this. She wrapped the Ace around his bicep. "That'll have to do."

Juliana led him to her bedroom, and he lay down on her bed. He was as docile as a lamb.

"Would you please strip me?" he asked.

Well, maybe a wolf in sheep's clothing. She shrugged. She'd seen him naked before. She pulled off his black sneakers, unsnapped and unzipped his black jeans, and pulled them and his black Jockeys down his long legs. His cock lay flaccid against his abdomen.

"Still not up for any hijinks I see," she joked.

His eyelids were heavy. "I won't leave you wanting this time, I promise."

Her heart turned over and her lower body tightened. "I'll hold you to that."

"I can't stay."

Hurt stabbed her.

"Will you come with me?"

Her heart seemed to flip in her chest. "To California?"

"To the Hilton." His eyes closed.

"What?"

"I have to bring my wife back with me. Tonight." His words slurred.

"Wife? What wife?"

But Charlie was dead to the world.

••••

Charlie woke with a jerk when Juliana removed the Band-Aid from his arm. His blue eyes were wide with fear until he saw her. Then he released a breath and sagged into her mattress.

"Who did you think I was?" she asked.

"Montgomery's men."

"You want to tell me what happened? It might take your mind off what I'm doing."

Charlie was a natural actor, but Juliana would swear in court he wasn't acting when he described the pursuit after he'd been shot. He'd been in mortal terror.

"I don't think about what I do now as being dangerous," he told her. "I locate things and people, I do errands for people, and I learn things for people. I help people."

"You mean being a private detective," she said.

"Yeah. After Billy died I felt … well … lots of things. Empty, useless, wasted."

Juliana stopped opening a sterile pad. "Wasted?"

Charlie's eyes were full of pain when he looked at her. "I never did anything with my life. I didn't become famous or a big star. Nobody recognizes my name or face out there. I'm one of thousands just like me—somebody who thought they could act and found out differently when they got to Hollywood."

"You're a wonderful actor. I watched you portray characters for years."

He gave her a sad smile. "Here I'm wonderful. There … well, the best are a lot better than I am. Everybody's beautiful out there. Everybody's got a hot body, great hair, you name it. I'm nothing special."

"But Charlie—" Juliana began to protest.

Charlie squeezed her arm. "I live there, you don't. You don't know what my life was like every day. I'm a little fish in a big pond. I'm wasted. Not like Billy. Billy was going to be somebody. He was going to cure cancer; he told me so. He had a great job in a research lab. He loved what he was doing. It was important work, work that was supposed to save lives. But somebody killed him."

"I'm sorry we didn't attend the funeral. We were in Mexico visiting family when it happened. We didn't hear until we returned.

I hated that I missed you." She knew about regrets. "I wish you'd stayed in Miami longer."

"So I could feel more guilt? Listen to more comments about how terrible it was that Billy died? He asked me to go with him to New Orleans but I had to shoot some stupid commercial. I don't even remember what it was for now. Selling some stupid product like air freshener or something. If I'd have gone with him, maybe he wouldn't have died. Maybe he wouldn't have been at that place at that time."

"You don't know that. Besides, Billy's death wasn't your fault."

"He needed me, and I didn't have time for him. My life was about pushing products people didn't need while Billy's was about making drugs people needed desperately."

"Not everybody is good at science," Juliana said.

"I'm good at nothing!" he snarled, then burst out, "It should have been *me*."

She gripped his hand. "Charlie, no!"

"Yes. Billy was important. I'm not."

Juliana was rocked to the core. "Everyone has value."

"Not me. Not then. So I gave it up, all of it. I couldn't bring Billy back, but I could do something of value. I knew a lady who'd lost her dog. It sounds stupid, but I started with that. She loved that dog. And I found it for her. She referred me to someone else who needed help. They referred me, too. I went to P.I. school and learned what I needed to help a lot more people. Sometimes it's little stuff, but I don't feel like I'm wasting my life now. I'll never be what Billy would have been, but I'm better than I was."

Juliana taped off the bandage. She didn't look at him. There'd been pain in every word, pain that resonated inside her with her own unfulfilled dreams. She'd spent so much time grieving and angry that she couldn't become a cop that she'd never considered any other way she might help people.

What he thought about himself was wrong, but he wouldn't believe her if she told him so. Grief did strange things to people. Look at her father, protecting her like a child long after she'd grown up.

But in essence, Charlie had killed himself to arise from the ashes as someone else. She'd thought because he smiled the same that he *was* the same, but he was different inside. Hurting, though he'd never admit it, vulnerable, needy, lonely. How she knew that last, she couldn't say, but she knew it intuitively.

Juliana lifted her gaze. "Is that why you won't call Rick?"

Charlie nodded. "The wrong brother died. But they can't see what I've done to atone."

His words slammed into her like bullets. "They can't know if you don't tell them."

"They won't believe me. You didn't."

"I'm sorry. I thought I knew you so well." But she didn't know this Charlie at all.

"I'm not that man anymore. I use parts of him in my job, that's all. When I'm successful, they'll have to believe."

She wanted—needed—to comfort him, but she didn't think he'd accept it. Not overtly given, at least. She collected the tape and bandages and returned them to the shopping bag. "That bandage should be changed every few hours. Can you do it yourself or do you want to come back here so I can take care of it?"

Charlie sat up, holding his arm against his chest and swung his legs over the side of the bed. He looked like a sultan with his dark hair and tanned skin. Hunger stirred in her lower body.

"I need you to come with me," he said.

"To take care of your wound?"

"No." He shook his head. "To find the sculpture."

"You can't go back there!"

"I can if I attend the wedding. Me and my wife."

"You said that before. What are you talking about?"

"I'm Joseph Castleton. You're my wife, Camille. The Castletons are real people. We're out-of-town guests of the Montgomerys staying at the Hilton."

"You're crazy. They'll know we're not the Castletons."

"They won't. They've invited five hundred people. They won't know everybody by sight. We'll be transported with the other guests and no one will be the wiser."

"What if—"

Charlie stood and wavered for a moment. Juliana slipped an arm around him to steady him. He gave her a sheepish grin. "I have to return to the Hilton tonight, and you have to come with me. I'm probably a danger on the road and I'm unsteady on my feet. Besides, you want to get into that wedding as much as I do."

Juliana bit her lip. It was true. She did want the sculpture. And she was worried about Charlie's current state.

"I need you, Juliana."

She stared into his blue eyes. Knowing what she did now, she thought he might not realize how much he needed her. And she admitted it; she needed to be needed by him.

"All right. Sit back down while I pack."

He did, with alacrity. "What kind of fancy dresses do you have?" He was unselfconscious about his nudity.

She had to clear her throat and tear her gaze away. "I have a few."

"Show me."

She pulled out her "little black dress." It had a flounce at the knees, for dancing. It plunged in a deep ruffled V-neck.

Charlie shook his head. "Next."

She pulled out her red sheath dress with the red beaded bolero. "It has a hat."

"That one has potential."

He rejected a flowered dress, a two-piece beige suit, and her short, sexy red-and-black salsa dress. His eyes widened and he licked his lips at a fringed off-one-shoulder, off-one-hip, melon-colored dancing dress.

"It reminds me of the skirt you had on yesterday when we made love," he said.

Her lower body heated with desire. Without her willing it, she looked at his lap, where his cock was showing signs of life. She tore her gaze away. His eyes glittered with sensual knowledge of what they'd shared together when they were naked.

Juliana shuddered and turned back to her closet. The final dress still had tags on it. She held it against her body as she stood before the full-length mirror. It was a knee-length sleeveless cream V-neck, the material shirred below her breasts into a diamond-shaped jewel. She gathered up her hair with her free hand, frowning.

"It's perfect!" Charlie exclaimed with enthusiasm from behind her, adding, "Camille."

"Are you sure? It wasn't expensive."

"It's the small touches that make people think you paid more for it. Do you have diamond jewelry?"

"Yes."

"Good. We'll have to hope no one notices we don't have wedding rings."

"I've got my parents' rings. My papá gave them to me before he married my *Tía* Dolores." She rooted in her jewelry box.

"Your dad married your aunt?"

She lifted her head. "My mamá's sister. I stayed with her after, you know, my dad caught us, until my papá moved near her. We were over there all the time. And one thing led to another. I've got two little half-brothers now." She shrugged. "She's a great stepmother, although I still think of her as my *tía*. Here," she handed him her father's thick gold band.

Juliana slipped on her mother's rings, a more delicate pair of interlocking bands with a large round diamond. She held her hand out for him to see. "Not ostentatious. My father bought them in Europe on his way back from the Korean War."

Charlie swallowed. "I think Camille has a practical streak." He slipped her father's ring on his hand. It was very loose.

"My dad's a bigger man than you."

Charlie looked up and smiled that sexy grin. "There you go demeaning my manhood again."

"I've found your manhood to be absolutely perfect."

His blue eyes heated. "I wish we had time to see how perfect, but we need to get to the Hilton while it's still dark. The fewer people who see us arrive the better."

"Can I get a rain check?" she asked.

"Absolutely."

When they arrived at the Hilton with Juliana's luggage in tow, Charlie insisted they enter through the front lobby.

"I thought the less people who saw us the better," Juliana said.

"We had a little too much to drink at the party we attended. If I'm unsteady on my feet, the party will account for it. If you laugh out loud, it will help our cover story. And if I get a little amorous, all the more reason for us to hang the 'Do Not Disturb' sign on the door."

"You're really good at this."

"Wait'll we get to the room and I show you how good I am." He waggled his eyebrows suggestively. "Ready?"

"Yes." She slid her free arm around his waist. He pulled her suitcase. She carried her garment bag.

They staggered into the lobby. Juliana had changed into white capris, a peach off-the-shoulder top and white high-heeled sandals. With Charlie leaning into her, there was every reason to teeter.

"C'mon, only a little further and then you can lie down," Juliana coaxed, in character.

Charlie leaned more of his weight against her and she had to shift to keep them both upright. Was he feeling light-headed or just playacting?

"I'm not drunk," he slurred so perfectly that anyone within hearing distance would know he was. "I'm just feeling good."

"C'mon, darling. Let's go to bed."

Charlie's smile was so damn sexy it curled her toes. "I love it when you talk dirty." Then he kissed her long and deep. This time her panties curled. Their room was too far away. Maybe she'd attack him in the elevator.

A man cleared his throat nearby. Juliana broke apart from Charlie trying to orient her mind. She had to remind herself they were playacting. Until they reached their room, at least.

A bellhop stood beside them. "Would you like help with your luggage?" The young Latino looked like he was fighting a smile.

"If you would." Juliana handed him her garment bag and took her suitcase from Charlie's lax grip, turning that over as well. She slid her arm around Charlie's waist and headed him to the elevator.

He nuzzled her neck while they waited and caressed her back from her neck to her buttocks the whole ride up to their floor. Her nerve endings sent urgent messages to her lower body and made her panties wet. Her nipples pebbled in the air conditioning.

"We should have come back hours ago, Camille," Charlie murmured.

"Joe, behave yourself for a few more minutes."

The bellhop did smile then.

They made it to the room. Charlie tipped the bellhop and Juliana managed to remind him, "Would you put on the 'Do Not Disturb' sign please and tell the front desk to hold our calls."

But the door had no sooner closed then Charlie gripped her to him for a fierce kiss. Full frontal press showed her he was primed and ready to go. Her body felt needy. She ached to feel his deep thrusts. It seemed a long time since they'd been joined.

Charlie maneuvered them to the bed. All the time his lips sucked at hers with hungry, urgent need. His hands delved under her blouse and closed over her aching breasts. It felt so good she cried out into his mouth. She tugged his shirt out of his pants and unsnapped his black jeans. When she lowered his zipper, he hissed. She rose on her toes as he stroked her nipples with his thumbs. Still, their lips clung together. She wanted their lower bodies mated, too.

She pushed his jeans and underwear down. As he kicked them away, she gripped his erect cock in both hands. It was hot and silky smooth. She caressed it with worshipping hands.

Charlie worked her out of her capris and panties. Together they pulled her shirt over her head and threw off his blazer and T-shirt. His gaze burned with desire.

Then he pushed her down on the bed and followed her. Juliana opened her legs to receive him, and he plunged inside.

"God," he groaned, adjusting his body on hers and pushing harder into her. "I've needed this all day."

Juliana wrapped her arms around him and pressed her hips upward. Charlie thrust hard and deep. She needed this joining, needed to finish what they'd begun earlier today. She met each thrust with her own.

"So good," he panted.

It was rough, it was urgent. Their bodies slapped together. "Hurry, Jules. I can't hold on." He thrust deep.

Her orgasm washed over her and drew him in. They strained together as their bodies convulsed, clutching each other.

Then the moment ended. They collapsed, panting.

"I can't get enough of you," he panted.

"Let me catch my breath and you can have me again."

Charlie lifted his head and caught her face between his hands. His blue eyes were nearly black. "I want to try to get into the house with the florist or the caterer. They both make deliveries in the morning. I don't know when exactly. Will you go with me?"

"All right."

He kissed her hard. "I need you."

"You have me."

"This might be our last night together."

"Then we'd better make the most of it."

"I don't want to sleep." He began to move inside her and he was hard and full once more.

"I don't want to sleep either."

Juliana clutched Charlie to her as he began to thrust slow and deep. She'd never had a connection like she had when she made love with him. And she didn't want it to end.

CHAPTER 12

Salsa music jerked Juliana awake, but something heavy prevented her from moving. Awareness identified the weight as Charlie pinning her to the bed, his hands entwined with hers on either side of her head. He was still buried deep in her body. She must have dozed off after they'd made love that last time. The clock read nine-thirty.

"What is it?" Charlie tightened his hold on her. His voice was groggy.

"My cell phone." It continued to play music.

"Ignore it." He shifted on her and in her, testing the size of his erection, which was growing larger.

"It's nine-thirty. What time are those deliveries? Hadn't we better get up?"

"I'm up." His erection was hard now, and he filled her.

Her cell phone quieted. "As much as I want to make love to you again, Charlie, if we can get the sculpture before the wedding, it would be better."

"Better than making love?" He thrust deep.

"No. But safer." It came out a squeak. "Couldn't we make love in the shower to move things along?" Her cell phone began to play again.

"Insistent bugger," he grumbled.

His grip on her tightened to near pain and he pressed fully inside her. Then he stilled as they both listened to the phone. His breaths were audible. His body quivered with tension. The world was intruding on their idyll, and they both knew what needed to be done.

"I don't want to stop," he said.

"I don't either, but if it's safer to go in with the florist or caterer, we have to try."

Still, he fought his body.

"We'll still be able to make love in the shower," she reminded him.

Charlie withdrew slowly from her body, leaving her feeling empty inside. He helped her from the bed. Her hips ached.

As he headed for the bathroom, she grabbed her cell phone from the nightstand. "Hello?"

"Juliana, it's Detective Montoya."

"Hello, Detective."

Charlie turned and gave her a sharp look.

"I was able to get a press pass for the wedding," Montoya said. "But still no luck on getting a photo. However, after last night it's more important than ever we get that relic off the market."

Her breath caught. "What happened last night?"

"Didn't you hear the news this morning?"

"No, I slept in."

"There was a shootout at a crack house. Two cops were killed before the perps blew up the house. One more was hurt in the explosion."

"Oh no! Any of your department?"

"No, another precinct. But we all feel it when men in blue go down. We can't have more of that shit pouring into the city. I know you understand. Can't you try to find the relic without a photo? Won't you try?"

Juliana closed her eyes and sighed. "I know what the relic looks like." She opened her eyes to see betrayal in Charlie's.

"How?" Detective Montoya demanded.

"I've been helping Detective Ziffkin's brother find a stolen object. It's the relic."

"My God, what luck. Then we have nothing to worry about. I'll drop the press pass at your house … "

"I may not need it. We're going to try to recover it now."

"The wedding's not for hours. What are you doing?"

"I can't tell you that. I'll call you later."

"Juliana, don't do anything stupid."

"I'll let you know how it goes."

Juliana hung up and turned to face Charlie. He was so sexy that she ached for him. But his expression was closed. "Two police officers were killed last night and another wounded. The narcotics officers need to make sure the statue doesn't get auctioned. Enough cops are killed every year fighting against drugs. We don't need more of them to die."

"So I became expendable." He said it in a flat tone.

"I didn't betray you."

"It sure sounded like it."

"All I said was the relic was the same thing you were looking for."

"And I told you they have no right to it. It belongs to my client. They can't just take it because they think it's the right thing to do." He stood with his fists clenched, the muscles in his bare body tensed. "I need a shower. We'd better get started if we're going to meet the florist or caterer's delivery." He turned and headed for the bathroom.

"Charlie."

He halted, his back stiff. She couldn't help noticing his firm, round, grabbable butt. Their bodies and hearts had been in harmony for hours as they made love. Now there was discord, and she hated it.

She moved closer and touched his back. He stiffened. "Charlie. I don't want to hurt you."

He remained silent for a moment, still tense. "You shouldn't have mentioned Rick's name."

It wasn't the response she'd expected. "I thought it gave you validation."

"He has nothing to do with this. You knew I didn't want him involved."

From bad to worse. What was driving him wouldn't allow him to divert from his path. "I'm sorry." It was all she could say.

Charlie stayed frozen for a moment. Then he gave a long sigh. "Come on. We need to shower."

"We?" She couldn't hide the hope in her voice.

"Yeah. I've got this need … "

"I'm interested."

•••

Juliana had betrayed him. The thought kept returning to Charlie's brain. They'd missed the caterers because they'd spent too long in the shower. He'd tried to forget her betrayal in her body, and their coupling had gotten out of control. Already a bruise in the shape of his hand had formed on her right bicep. It would be visible in the beautiful cream dress. God, this had to work so they wouldn't have to attend the wedding. He felt the clock ticking in his brain. He had to get the sculpture now before the narcs tried to stop him from taking it to California.

He and Juliana waited in the car outside the florist, dressed in jeans and T-shirts. She had her hair in a ponytail and wore heavy mascara and eyeliner, dark eye shadow, and black lipstick. Goth didn't begin to describe her. She looked years younger than she was. He'd let his hair air dry, so it curled riotously, and had pulled locks forward onto his forehead. He looked like he was in his twenties again.

Charlie checked to be sure his bandage was hidden under his shirt's sleeve. He couldn't let it show at the Montgomery mansion. The wounds throbbed from this morning's exertions. He rubbed his chest where Juliana had bitten him. He liked wearing her marks of possession.

"There." Juliana pointed as the florist van pulled up to the back door of the shop.

They exited Juliana's car and approached the van. One of the employees looked up. "Mr. Montgomery said we should help," Charlie said.

"Talk to the manager." The dark-haired young man jerked a thumb over his shoulder. "Maggie Solomon."

Charlie and Juliana walked over to Maggie, a middle-aged blonde woman. Again, Charlie gave his cover story.

"We have enough help." Maggie continued shoving papers onto a clipboard.

"He's paying us, so we're supposed to work," Charlie said.

Maggie's dark gaze sharpened. "*He's* paying you?"

"Yeah. My dad works for him. I'm John. This is my girlfriend, Sondra. We got delayed."

Maggie looked them over, her gaze lingering a moment on Juliana's bruise and the love bite on her exposed midriff. "I see. Okay, you can help. We need to load all the flowers for the wedding into the vans, take them out to the estate, place the ones in the house, and store the rest in the coolers."

"We can do that," Juliana said.

The loading completed, Charlie and Juliana had to sit on the floor in one of the vans. Surrounded by blooms, the sweet odor was nearly overpowering. He kept his arm around her and nuzzled the side of her face. It was part of their cover, but he couldn't stop touching her. He wanted to kiss her, but for them, kissing was a prelude to making love.

There was another reason Charlie kept physical contact with Juliana. She was like a GPS device using the sculpture photo in her jeans pocket as her destination. Her body was tight with tension, like a violin string, and when they pulled up to the Montgomery gates, she inhaled sharply.

He did kiss her then, and whispered in her ear. "Keep calm."

She nodded and kissed him back.

Now *his* body hummed with tension. He couldn't be near her without wanting to be inside her.

The van pulled close to the back door.

Maggie had to call Juliana's fake name twice to get her attention. The florist handed her a tall vase of beautiful gladioli and gave her directions to the front foyer. She handed another wider vase to Charlie. "Living room coffee table. Through the foyer. Follow her."

When they entered the house, Juliana whispered. "It's here."

"Where?" In his excitement, he had trouble keeping his voice down.

"Wait." Juliana closed her eyes to slits.

Charlie nudged her down the hallway. He didn't want to attract attention to them.

The hallway widened onto a beautiful two-story marble foyer. A wide, curved staircase led to the upper floors.

Juliana pulled up short near the stairs, her eyes opening. "Up."

Dammit, there were people upstairs. The risk of discovery was high if they attempted the second floor. From where he stood, Charlie could see the living room filled with beautiful furnishings and artwork. Damn Montgomery for stealing the sculpture. Some men could never have enough money.

Charlie and Juliana placed their vases. She eyed the staircase, licking her lips.

He watched the movement with hunger burning in his gut, and lower. He wrenched his gaze away. Should they attempt the upper floors? After getting shot he felt some trepidation for himself. He felt even more for Juliana. He had to protect her.

"Well, what are you waiting for?" Maggie demanded from behind them. "There's more to unload." She moved past them to adjust the flowers in the vase Juliana had placed.

Charlie guided Juliana back to the vans.

"Can we get upstairs?" she whispered.

"It's risky. I'll think about it while we unload. Tell me if the sculpture moves during that time."

Maggie didn't give them any other flowers for the front of the house. Charlie saw a back staircase as they loaded exquisite red roses into the cooler. They were almost done unloading. If they were going to risk it, they had to do it now.

But Haley Montgomery, the bride herself, descended the back staircase looking annoyed. Charlie drew Juliana to him and ducked his face against her neck. He didn't think Montgomery's daughter paid much attention to the help around her, but he couldn't take any chances.

"Miss Montgomery," Maggie greeted the girl. "Would you like to see your bouquet? It's gorgeous."

"Sure." Haley followed Maggie to the cooler.

"Up," Charlie urged Juliana. They had to try for the sculpture.

They made it up the stairs, but in the hallway they saw a blonde woman with her back to them. Charlie dragged Juliana back into the stairwell.

"It's that way," Juliana pointed down the hall.

Female voices came from below. Maggie and Haley returning. Dammit. "Down," Charlie ordered.

"But we're close," Juliana protested.

"Close to getting caught. Move."

They made it to the bottom of the stairs before the two women appeared. Charlie took Juliana in his arms for a hungry kiss.

"Back to the van you two." Maggie sounded resigned.

Charlie tugged Juliana away from the stairs, from the house, from the sculpture. They'd have to try again during the wedding. And they'd have to succeed.

CHAPTER 13

Charlie drove Juliana's car behind the limo from the hotel to the wedding, giving the other guests the excuse they couldn't stay for the entire reception due to another commitment later that evening.

Juliana felt wired. This was it, their last chance to reclaim the sculpture before some drug scumbag bought it to create a drug empire in Miami.

Charlie said the sculpture would probably be downstairs this time, easier to reach. She hoped so. Her nerves couldn't take an extended search for it.

There was a line of cars in front of them turning into the estate, and parked cars lined the curb.

"This will work to our advantage," Charlie said. "We can park in the street for a quick getaway." He flashed her a smile.

Juliana wished they had a concrete plan instead of contingencies based on what-ifs. Bank robbers had better-laid plans than she and Charlie. Did he always fly by the seat of his pants? As a boy he'd been restless, flitting from dream to dream. He hadn't liked to stand still, and he didn't like structure. What was he like now?

They had to park half a dozen houses down the road. They joined the other wedding guests heading for the gate.

"You look stunning in that dress, darling," Charlie said.

Juliana smiled at him. He'd said the same thing in their hotel room, only with much more heat. She'd been surprised at how sophisticated she looked in the dress with her hair in a French twist. Charlie looked very Californian dressed in dark slacks, dark blazer, and a cerulean shirt with a Mandarin collar. The expensive sunglasses were a nice touch. He looked very sexy.

She had her hand looped through his right arm. They gave their cover names to a guard at the gate, who checked his list and let them through.

She exhaled a sigh of relief.

The guests headed for the house. Juliana tightened her hold on Charlie's arm. This was it. She had the photo in the silver purse on her shoulder. As she crossed the threshold, she gripped it tight.

Dalton Montgomery and his wife were greeting guests a few feet inside the door. Juliana's breath caught. How were she and Charlie going to get past the man?

Yet Charlie held her in line until it was their turn. Charlie gripped Montgomery's hand. "A beautiful day for a wedding."

"Yes," Juliana added. "Thank you for inviting us."

"Welcome to our home." Montgomery studied them, trying to identify them. "Please have some champagne."

Charlie towed Juliana further into the foyer where a server offered them flutes of champagne, which he refused. She led him into the spacious living room where other guests mingled. When they were in front of the second hallway, her body turned toward it. She smiled at Charlie and lowered her voice. "Down that hall."

With studied nonchalance, he turned. A smile lit his face. He dropped his head to nuzzle her ear. "As I suspected. I know the way in there. When the ceremony begins, we need to be in the house."

"Wonderful," she said in a normal tone.

"Let's mingle a little. I don't want to attract attention."

Charlie proved adept at conversing with strangers. He simply asked people questions about themselves. He and Juliana gave their cover names if asked, usually just their first names. And the lies he told—he was an independent film producer, small but expecting to grow; he was an architect, he was a stock trader, he owned an import-export company.

Where he came up with the whopper that Juliana was pregnant with their first child she didn't know, but it allowed most of the women to cluck over her and give her advice. She barely had to say a word.

After several of these conversations, she began to daydream about what it would be like to have a child. *Charlie's* child. Dark-haired, with her dark eyes. His son would be a heartbreaker ... like him.

A slender blonde woman in a mint green silk dress made her way through the room. "If everyone would move into the back yard and find a seat, we'll begin the wedding."

The couples Juliana and Charlie had been talking to headed toward the foyer. Charlie held her back from following, instead grabbing a glass of champagne. He watched the hallway nearest them with feigned indifference. After a few minutes a couple headed that way and Charlie followed them.

The sculpture pulled like it was tied to her with a rope. Charlie held her to a slow pace, his arm around her waist. He had to feel her body trembling.

When they reached a doorway on her left, she gasped.

"Breathe, Camille."

She clutched his arm. "In here."

"As I suspected," he whispered. Louder, he said, "Here, hold onto me."

Juliana heard more people in the hall behind them. Frustration gripped her. The sculpture was right in front of them but they couldn't get to it.

Charlie pulled her forward. The couple in front of them was already out of sight, but he seemed to know the way. Of course, he'd been here last night.

They entered a large indoor patio. The furniture all faced the green lawn where a large white tent stood, the blue ocean providing a gorgeous backdrop. Guests filled hundreds of white chairs. White-haired women were taking seats indoors.

"Perhaps you should stay out of the sun if you're feeling faint," Charlie suggested aloud. "You wouldn't want to cause a stir during the ceremony."

Several women looked their way. "She's pregnant," Charlie told them, his face glowing. The women gave her knowing smiles.

Why was he drawing attention to them? How were they going to slip away unnoticed?

The music began, and the crowd inside quieted. Everyone focused behind the chairs. The bride appeared wearing a gorgeous white silk gown, and there were exclamations of appreciation from the crowd.

Charlie leaned toward her. "You're going to feel sick. Frown and clutch your stomach."

She nodded, doing as she was told. He pulled her from her chair, and they headed toward the door. When they were in the hallway, Charlie said aloud, "I know we passed a bathroom. Hold on."

Juliana followed him to the left. But as they neared the kitchen, she could hear people talking. It had to be the caterers. Charlie flattened against the wall and peered around the doorway. He held his hand up to wait, then signaled her to move toward the hall on her right. She walked on her toes to limit her high-heeled sandals from clicking on the floor.

When they reached the room with the sculpture, she felt nearly faint with relief. Charlie let her pass him. She went to the large mahogany desk and her hand reached out to touch the bottom drawer. "In here."

Charlie produced lock picks and got the drawer open. Moments later he opened the door of the safe. Inside was an object wrapped in cloth. She reached past Charlie to touch it. Her hand tingled.

"Yes," she sighed.

He unwrapped the object. It was smaller than she'd expected, about the size of a paperback book. The carving was very detailed. He placed it in her hands while he returned the cloth, locked the safe and the drawer.

The sculpture's violent history swamped her, and she swayed beneath the onslaught. She shoved the information to the back of her mind, where it was like a dull buzzing. She couldn't afford to be distracted now. They had to hide it. She should have brought a bigger purse.

Charlie tugged his shirt from his pants and the action drew her attention. What was he doing? He'd pushed the door nearly closed. Was he planning to have sex *now*? *Here*?

He produced a small roll of black electrical tape from his jacket pocket and handed it to her. "Tape it to my chest."

"What?"

"It's the safest way to get it out of here. Hurry."

He held the sculpture in place while she circled him, taping it to his chest. The black tape made almost no noise when she pulled it from the roll.

"Several more times," he ordered.

Juliana did as instructed with shaking hands. Any moment she expected the door to fly open and Montgomery's men to rush in with guns drawn.

"Enough?" she whispered.

Charlie tested it. "Yeah." He tucked his shirt back in and stuck the tape back in his pocket.

"Now we leave. You're ill, remember?"

"Yes." She felt ill. They had to get away.

Charlie opened the office door and looked out. Then he wrapped his arm around Juliana. She laid her head against his chest as they walked toward the living room.

Juliana didn't remember the hall being this long, the living room so wide, or the foyer so deep. Then they were outside. The hot sun beating down on her couldn't warm the cold pit of fear inside her. It seemed to take forever to reach the gate, yet all at once it loomed in front of her.

"My wife is feeling ill. I'm sorry to leave so soon," Charlie told the guard.

Juliana murmured, "Honey, please."

"Hold on. You can lie down in the car."

Then they were on the street. Her nerves screamed at her to run. Her back felt hot, like it was branded with a target.

The walk took forever. Any minute she expected a shout from Montgomery's guards. Her body trembled against Charlie's.

"Hold on," he reassured her.

At last they reached the car. "Stay in character," Charlie warned her, "in case they're watching."

She allowed him to help her into the car and recline her seat. Sweat beaded on her forehead and at the back of her neck. He started the car and pulled out of their parking spot. The car accelerated. Juliana held her breath. Were they going to get away?

"No pursuit, but stay down." He sounded calm but his knuckles were white on the steering wheel.

When they'd gone several miles, he flexed his fingers. "You can sit up now."

Juliana raised the seat and let the air conditioning blow full force on her. "God, that was nerve-wracking. I feel drained."

Charlie flashed her a smile. "But I bet you never felt more alive."

"True." Since he'd walked back into her life.

"I'm going to drop you at your apartment, get my car, and then I'm going straight to the airport."

Disappointment swamped her. "Won't they be looking for you there?"

"With security nowadays, they won't be able to bring guns into the airport. And they won't know what airline I'm using. I'll change my appearance."

She wanted to beg him to wait a few days but knew her motives were selfish; she hadn't had enough of Charlie Ziffkin. She feared she never would.

Too soon they entered her apartment's parking lot. These were their last moments together, and all of them would be public ones. No making love for the final time. She gulped back tears. She'd known all along this moment was coming. She'd been a fool to give Charlie her heart again.

Juliana caught her breath. Had she lost her heart to him? She'd thought they were having an affair. No, he'd always had her heart. She'd given it to him when she was thirteen, long before she'd offered him her body, and she'd never taken it back. She was such a fool. She loved him.

Charlie pulled into her parking spot. "We made it."

"Yeah." Juliana climbed out and watched as he opened her trunk. He grabbed his luggage. Charlie traveled light, mostly clothes to slip into his different personas.

Juliana knew her heart was in her eyes. She felt the stupid tears and tried to will them away. Charlie hadn't asked for her heart. He hadn't asked for more than to share her body, and she'd given that willingly.

He looked up from his bags and froze. "Jules. Juliana. Don't." He dropped his bags.

Juliana stepped into his opening arms. His mouth descended to hers.

"Freeze! Miami P.D.!"

CHAPTER 14

Charlie's arms closed around Juliana as two plainclothes cops with guns surrounded them. His mind raced. These had to be Juliana's narcs. They wanted the sculpture. Her betrayal had found him at last.

"Let go of the woman," one barked.

Charlie gripped her harder, the sculpture pressed into both their bodies, a reminder of what was at stake.

"I've committed no crime," Charlie said.

"Charlie," Juliana begged.

"Say nothing."

"Shut up, Ziffkin. I said let her go," the dark-haired Latino cop ordered.

"You're not going to risk Captain Sanchez's daughter," Charlie said.

"Charlie." Juliana squirmed. It should have been erotic, but with the sculpture grinding into his chest, it wasn't. "Detective Montoya, stop this nonsense."

So it *was* Juliana's narcs.

"We want the relic. It's too important to leave in this amateur's hands," Montoya responded.

"I don't have any relic, and I don't have anything that belongs to the Miami P.D.," Charlie said. "You're making a mistake pointing guns at an innocent civilian."

"This is no mistake. Juliana, move away from him," Montoya ordered.

"Don't move," Charlie pleaded. He saw the torn loyalty in her face. Could she break a lifetime's conditioning of being a policeman's daughter?

Her look of anguish crushed that hope. She jerked against his wounded arm. Charlie grunted in pain, his arm contracted toward his chest, and she slid from his grasp.

Instantly the two cops were on him, spinning him against the car. One of them jammed a gun into his neck.

"I said freeze, dirt bag!" Montoya snarled.

"Detective Montoya, there's no reason to use force," Juliana protested.

The other cop jerked Charlie's arms up behind his back. Fresh pain stabbed through his wounds, but he gritted his teeth to prevent a groan.

"You're under arrest," the second cop said.

Juliana gasped. "For what?"

"Obstruction of justice." Detective Montoya kept pressure on the gun at Charlie's neck.

His partner snapped handcuffs on Charlie's wrists.

"That's ridiculous," she exclaimed. "Detective Montoya, put that gun away." There was steel in her voice. Amazingly, Montoya listened.

The other cop emptied Charlie's jacket pockets, but when he tried to frisk him, Juliana slid between the two men, pressing against Charlie's body.

"Detective Hunt, that's completely unnecessary. I swear to you on my mother's grave he's not armed."

"Juliana, get out of the way," Montoya growled.

"No. I told you the truth. He's not armed."

Hunt managed to search around Juliana, but couldn't reach the middle of Charlie's chest where the statue was taped. Charlie grinned bitterly. Small mercies.

Hunt told his partner, "I got lock picks, a roll of tape, a wallet, and a set of keys."

Then he pulled Juliana off Charlie and spun him around. Charlie stared at Juliana.

Montoya kept his gun trained on Charlie. "Check the bags."

Hunt crouched and searched the bags. "Nothing. I'll check the car."

Charlie kept his gaze on Juliana, willing her not to say anything. She gripped her hands together as she watched the detectives. Her color was high. She'd already done more to protect him than he'd thought she would.

Detective Hunt returned looking angry. "Not there either. Maybe they didn't get it."

"They got it," Montoya snarled. "Where is it, Juliana?"

"Jules," Charlie begged.

Her brown eyes softened. Her lips parted. Without looking away from Charlie, she said, "I can't tell you."

"Juliana," Montoya snapped. "He can't hurt you. Tell us where it is."

"I'm not worried about Charlie hurting me. He's not a threat to anyone. There's no reason to handcuff him and hold him at gunpoint."

"Juliana, you're a cop's daughter. You know how important this evidence is to us. Cops are dying."

Anguish twisted Juliana's face. Charlie braced himself for her familial loyalties to snap into place. Her eyes pleaded with him. He would do anything for her … anything but this. He gave a small shake of his head.

She crossed her arms across her chest. "I plead the fifth."

Charlie sagged with relief. She hadn't betrayed him … again.

"You're coming to the precinct with us." Montoya's voice was a growl of anger. "And I'm putting a call into your father, Juliana."

Several emotions chased across her face—shock, fear, and then mulish determination. "Fine."

The cops closed her trunk, grabbed Charlie's bags, and loaded him and Juliana into the back seat of their nondescript sedan.

"Charlie, I'm sorry," she whispered.

"Don't talk to him, Juliana," Montoya ordered.

Her chin lifted. "Are you all right?" she asked in a louder voice.

"Yeah. Arrested twice in one week. Miami cops sure know how to show a guy a good time."

"Twice?" Detective Hunt asked, craning around the seat back.

Charlie ignored him. He didn't have long to win Juliana's support. He needed her help to escape this trap. She'd been raised with the moral right of law enforcement. He'd use that against the two detectives. "It's strange, don't you think, Jules, that I've been arrested more times than Montgomery."

"Stop it," she chided. "Hunt and Montoya aren't the bad guys."

"I'm not either. But they're sure treating me like I am. False arrest isn't a charge to be taken lightly."

"Neither is obstructing justice," Montoya said from the driver's seat. "Now shut up."

"You think he's feeling guilty about something?" Charlie's arm throbbed from the pressure of his cuffed hands behind him. "He crossed a line, Jules, you know that. Are you going to condone his behavior?"

"Shut up," Montoya repeated.

"Did your papá ever cross the line like that, Juliana? Sergeant Sanchez was all about right and wrong, wasn't he?"

"Charlie … "

"He wanted to whup me himself that day he caught us, but he let my dad do it because that was the right thing to do."

Juliana's eyes widened with surprise. "Your dad beat you?"

"Hell, yes. I didn't touch another girl till senior year."

Her face softened. "I didn't know that."

"How could you, when you moved so far away?"

"It wasn't my choice."

"You know why I moved to California?" he asked her.

"To be an actor."

"Uh-uh. 'Cause you weren't there anymore."

Her eyes were huge with uncertainty and pain. "Don't play," she whispered. Her face was inches from his.

"I'm not," he whispered back. "It hurt too much to look at your house and know you didn't live there anymore."

She leaned her head against his chest, and he nuzzled her hair. He caught Detective Hunt's wide-eyed look. *Take that, copper.*

The detectives installed him in an interrogation room, one with a two-way mirror, separating him from Juliana. After telling them he wouldn't say anything unless she was returned to him, he sat in the straight chair and endured an hour of badgering. But he said nothing.

Every minute they kept him here made it more dangerous for him to go to the airport, but he didn't let that show on his face. And every minute Juliana was separated from him was time for them to break her. He thought her father might be able to obtain the truth. Her family loyalty was strong.

There was a knock on the door. Charlie tensed. His heart raced. Had they broken her?

Montoya opened the door. "Thanks for coming." He moved aside.

"In trouble again, bro?" Rick asked.

Oh, shit.

• • •

Juliana faced her father across the scratched metal table in the interrogation room. She'd risen when he entered to face him on equal footing, literally and figuratively.

"Detective Montoya says you're withholding evidence," he accused.

"It's not evidence."

"Don't play word games with me, *m'hija*. This is police business. You tell them what they need to know."

Juliana crossed her arms across her chest. "I can't."

"Can't? Because you're sleeping with Charlie Ziffkin?"

"No! Yes. No."

"Which is it?" he demanded.

"What I do with Charlie in the privacy of my home is no one's business, including yours."

He waved that away with a big hand. "This isn't about him."

"Isn't it? You're angry not only because I have a lover but because it's Charlie."

"This is about evidence."

"Right. That's why they sent for my *father*. I'm not a little girl anymore."

"These are adult charges we're talking about."

"Nobody's charged me with anything. Because I'm not guilty of anything. And neither is Charlie. Talk about trumped-up charges."

"You listen to me, *m'hija*—"

"No, you listen to me, *Captain Sanchez*. Charlie's got a right to sue Miami P.D. for unlawful arrest, and if he does, I'll testify, truthfully, that Miami P.D. was wrong. Dead wrong. How will that look for a captain's daughter to be a star witness for the prosecution?"

Her father held his hands out to her. "How has he turned you against the department? His own brother is a detective with the force."

"Charlie is right, Papá. It's not illegal to be right."

"But the narcotics detectives need that evidence."

"Taking what doesn't belong to you is stealing, Papá, even when cops do it. You taught me that when I was a little girl."

He ran a hand through his mostly black hair. "You look lovely in that dress. Did you dress that way for *him*?"

"We went to the Montgomery wedding. I dressed the part."

His eyes narrowed. "It was a terrible risk for you to go there."

She raised her chin. "I judged the risk acceptable."

"You don't know anything. You could have been killed!"

"I know that. His guards are armed and use lethal force."

Her father paled. "How do you know that?"

Juliana shrugged. "All that matters is I didn't go there ignorant."

"And you got the relic?"

Juliana said nothing.

"I know you did," he persisted. "You can find anything. Where did he stash it, Juliana? Tell me."

She looked at him and felt the distance between them grow. They stood on opposite sides of the issue. She wanted to tell him. She didn't like to see herself changing in his eyes. But Charlie deserved her silence, so she said nothing.

"You owe me this. I'm your papá. I love you. Can you say the same about Charlie Ziffkin?"

No, she couldn't.

CHAPTER 15

Charlie faced his brother and acted for all he was worth. "This is false imprisonment. I could sue."

Rick sat down across the table from him. "You could give the detectives what they want."

"I guess blood isn't thicker than water."

Rick's face reddened. "Don't ever say that again."

"You chose to believe your cop buddies over me. What else should I think?" Charlie shrugged.

"When are you going to take this situation seriously?" Rick demanded. "This isn't some damn game. What the hell were you doing anywhere near Dalton Montgomery? You have no idea what kind of bad news that guy is."

"Yes I do."

"You haven't got a clue. You've been living out there in Hollywood so long you think life is like the movies, that bullets are fake."

Charlie stilled. His chest felt tight and it wasn't from the tape. "Yeah, like the knife that killed Billy wasn't real, and it was all a dream, and he'll be back in next week's episode. Right?"

Rick sucked in his breath. "Have you got a death wish?" Suddenly he reached across the table and before Charlie could elude him, grabbed his upper arms. Charlie shouted with pain.

Rick let loose. "What the hell?"

Charlie's breaths came fast. He thought he was going to be sick. His eyes had closed, and his head drooped. He gripped the arm to his chest. He heard his brother coming around the table. Charlie should get up and move away.

When he heard Rick beside him, Charlie said through gritted teeth, "Don't touch me. Police brutality."

"I'm not the police. I'm your brother."

Charlie opened his eyes just as Rick reached for his arm. His hand snaked out to grip his brother's wrist. "Get a warrant."

"That's not how it works between brothers."

"It does now."

"I'm bigger and stronger than you. I always have been. From what I can tell, you've got one good arm. I can take you."

The door opened and Detectives Montoya and Hunt entered.

"Three on one, eh?" Charlie quipped, although he didn't feel the situation funny.

"You can either take the jacket off, or these guys'll hold you down while I do."

"You're really looking for a lawsuit," Charlie said.

"Take the damn jacket off," Rick growled. "I want to see what's wrong with you."

Charlie debated. The jacket helped hide the sculpture. But he knew Rick. If his brother said he was going to get the jacket off, he would.

Charlie stood. The chair screeched back. Rick remained rooted, but the two narcs moved forward. He slipped his good arm out and then slid the jacket down the other arm to pool on the floor.

Rick hissed and reached for his arm, but Charlie yanked it away. "That's blood! What happened?"

"It's a love bite. I'm into S & M." Charlie dared not look away from his brother.

Rick stepped forward. "Let me see."

Charlie sidestepped. "Not a chance."

He noted Detective Hunt coming around to his side of the table. Charlie backpedaled until his back hit the wall. This was ridiculous. He was a thirty-year-old man and his brother was acting like they were kids again.

"I want a lawyer," Charlie said.

Montoya and Hunt froze, but Rick kept coming.

"Now," Charlie insisted.

"You're gonna get a phone call, but it's going to be to Mom." Rick grabbed Charlie's shoulder and ripped the sleeve off to expose the blood-soaked bandage.

"Shit." Rick grabbed Charlie's arm. With his other hand he blocked Charlie's free hand. "That's a fucking bullet wound! Exit wound on the other side," he said conversationally to the other detectives. His gaze rose to meet Charlie's. "Untreated and unreported."

Charlie set his teeth.

"And it happened since I saw you yesterday afternoon."

"Montgomery's men?" Montoya asked.

"And you went back there today?" Rick asked, his voice incredulous. "Are you stupid?"

Charlie glared at his brother.

"What time yesterday did this happen, before or after midnight?"

"Did you take Juliana with you?" Detective Hunt asked.

Charlie switched his glare to him.

"You put Juliana Sanchez in the line of fire?" Rick demanded.

Charlie's head snapped back to face his brother. "You think so little of me. You don't know anything about me. I would die for her."

• • •

Juliana's heart thudded madly in her chest. Charlie cared for her deeply. She'd heard enough through the two-way mirror. She whirled away from her father and headed for the interrogation room where she yanked open the door. The cops had Charlie cornered like some wild animal.

"You'd better take your hands off your brother, Rick. He's asked for a lawyer." She strode into their midst. Charlie's gaze lit on her in silent agony. She didn't think he'd wanted her to hear what he'd said. Why didn't he want her to know how he felt about her?

But his carefree smile crossed his face. She knew he was faking happiness.

"Did you know about this?" Rick indicated the wound.

"Did you know the detectives didn't read Charlie his rights? Whatever case they thought they had went right down the toilet."

"I'm his brother," Rick said. "Miranda doesn't apply to me."

"Oh? I hadn't realized Charlie was underage. When did that happen?"

"My *mom* made it happen. She told me to find out what Charlie was up to, and that's what I'm doing."

"I see you, your mom and my dad share the same failing. You won't accept we've grown up." Juliana pried Rick's hands off Charlie. Charlie's lip quirked up on one side. His blue eyes were dancing. He slid his uninjured arm around her waist.

She turned to face the detectives. "Now, do we really need a lawyer or are you going to let us walk out of here?"

Montoya stepped forward. "I was hoping you'd tell us where the relic was. We know for a fact you have it. Because we just got a report about violence at the Montgomery wedding. Dalton Montgomery was shot."

"What?" Charlie's arm tightened around her.

Juliana felt short of breath. "Is he dead?"

"He took a bullet to the chest. He was rushed to the hospital. His prognosis is unknown at this time."

"What happened?" Charlie asked.

"Shortly after the wedding ceremony ended, Montgomery went into his study with some of his 'guests,'" Montoya reported. "According to witnesses at the scene, one of those guests had had too much to drink, and an argument ensued. Knowing how valuable that relic is, apparently the man didn't like being betrayed. He shot Montgomery, and Montgomery's men killed him."

"So you see how urgent it is that we get that relic," Hunt added.

"Who's your client, Charlie?" Rick asked in a quiet voice. "Who did you risk your life for?"

"Why?" Juliana asked. "What's that got to do with Montgomery?"

"Detectives Montoya and Hunt told me how valuable that relic is … to drug dealers. What happened to Montgomery is an example. Is your client a drug dealer, Charlie?"

"No," Charlie answered.

"Are you sure?"

"He's a Hollywood promoter."

"Will you wait here while we run a check on him?"

"Now you're going to harass Charlie's client? Why?" Juliana demanded.

"Call it a gut feeling or call it cop's intuition," Rick replied. "I can't believe this guy just happened to have an item like this lying around."

Charlie looked at Juliana. She nodded. He sighed. "His name's Jordan Hessler."

"While you're waiting, you're going to have that arm looked at," his brother said.

Charlie shrugged. "Sure, why not."

The narcotics detectives left them alone with Rick and an EMT who promised to be discreet. Juliana held Charlie's hand as the EMT stitched up his arm.

"Thanks for what you did," Charlie whispered so his brother couldn't hear.

"I think you should give them what they want." She put her fingers on his lips to keep him from interrupting. "But it should be your choice to do it."

He kissed her fingers.

She glanced over her shoulder at Rick. "I see what you mean about your family. My father treated me like a child in the other room. I don't think I've ever grown up in his mind."

"You must have gotten him to see the light, because you came to me."

"I don't think I got that far with him. I think he wonders who the stranger is in his daughter's body."

Charlie smiled with heat in his eyes.

Juliana felt her cheeks burn. "That came out wrong."

His thumb drew circles on the inside of her palm. "The way you said it, that stranger would be me."

"You're not a stranger, not really."

"All finished," the EMT said. "When was your last tetanus booster?"

Charlie frowned. "I don't know. Five years ago, maybe."

"I'd better give you another one to be safe. And a shot of antibiotics. You're lucky this isn't already infected. Bullet wounds need proper treatment immediately."

Charlie grimaced. Rick walked over to check the wound.

"Ordinarily I give the antibiotics shot in the butt," the EMT said, surveying the onlookers.

"That's a two-way mirror over there," Charlie said. "I'd prefer not to be a peep show."

"OK, but it's gonna hurt."

"It already hurts."

"Don't say I didn't warn you."

When the EMT stuck the needle in the muscle near the wound, Charlie yelled. He bit his lip for the second shot. Then they thanked the EMT, who cleaned up his equipment and left.

Rick sat down in the chair he'd vacated. "You could have died if the bullet had hit you six inches to the right."

"But it didn't," Charlie said.

"I don't want to lose another brother."

Juliana saw the reminder of their brother's murder in both their eyes.

"I'm not as inept as you think, Rick," Charlie said. "They make you take classes before you can get your P.I. license."

"Classes don't cover everything. They don't teach you how to avoid a bullet."

"I did pretty well. I got away."

"This time." Rick's brown eyes were grave.

"Rick, I'm not looking for danger. I just try to do my job, whatever someone hires me to do."

"Do you vet your clients?"

"I don't do a background check, no. I get referrals mostly."

Rick leaned back in his chair. "This Jordan Hessler, he was referred to you?"

Charlie hesitated before answering. "He called me. Said he'd heard of my work."

"Did he say who referred him?"

"That was enough for me. I knew him from the industry."

"I see."

"Rick, it's no different than when people come to the cops for help. You don't vet them."

Rick opened his mouth to reply when Montoya and Hunt returned. They pulled up chairs and sat down across the table. Their faces were set and serious. Juliana braced herself and gripped Charlie's hand.

"There's good news and bad news," Montoya reported. "Your client doesn't have a record."

"And the bad news?" Charlie asked.

"The California narcs and the DEA suspect he supplies drugs in Hollywood."

CHAPTER 16

"Rumor in the drug community is there will soon be a new top man in town," Montoya reported. "His name is Jordan Hessler. Your client."

The news hit Charlie in his solar plexus. He'd been suckered by a Hollywood player. Jordan had known he wanted to promote his P.I. business and had offered it to him in exchange for retrieving the sculpture. He'd come to Miami an innocent, star-struck fool.

The sculpture dug into Charlie's chest. He wasn't returning it to an honest man. Jordan Hessler was the tool to flood Hollywood with more drugs.

Juliana squeezed his hand.

"You didn't know your client's reputation?" Montoya prompted.

Charlie started to shake his head, but then he realized he had known. "I'd heard rumors people could get drugs at his parties. You can't work out there without some idea of where you can get a buzz. But I didn't make the connection."

"Bro, he used you," Rick said.

Charlie sighed. "I know that." Disappointment weighed on him. And shame. His brother and Juliana were witnessing his failure.

"You going to give him a drug pipeline?" Montoya asked.

Charlie's free hand fisted. He'd taken a bullet for nothing. He'd risked Juliana for nothing. He'd been belligerent with the police—the real good guys—for nothing.

His shoulders slumped. "No."

"Where'd you stash the relic, Charlie?" Rick asked.

All for nothing. Charlie had changed his life so he could make a difference, make his family proud of him, make them value him the way they'd valued Billy. There must be a way to make a difference this time. Billy was probably killed by someone on drugs. Could Charlie use the statue to strike a blow against the drug world? Avenge Billy in some way?

"If I produce it," he began, "is there a way to use it to prove Jordan Hessler is a drug dealer?"

Montoya and Hunt looked at each other, and Montoya answered. "We're not familiar enough with the California drug community to answer that."

"Can your counterparts out there or the DEA tell me?"

"Probably." Montoya frowned. "You're proposing a trade?"

Charlie inhaled. "I'm proposing a sting. I've already got an in with Jordan. If I get on a plane now, I can be there before evening, before Montgomery gets out of surgery and can issue any orders, if he lives. They can wire me and get it on tape, whatever they need."

Montoya shook his head. "You're a civilian. The DEA isn't going to go for that."

"No, Charlie," Rick said.

Charlie shot to his feet. "I'm not a civilian. I'm a licensed private investigator. I've had training. I'm not useless. I can do this." He had to salvage something out of this and prove he was capable, that he could contribute.

"You were fumbling around on this end," Hunt reminded him.

"I know better now. You're concerned about some Columbian drug lord funneling drugs into your city. Hell, he's going to funnel them somewhere no matter what. Why not do a sting on *him*?" God, yes.

Juliana shook her head. He saw fear in her eyes. For him. Not her, too.

"Mr. Ziffkin, that's pretty naive," Montoya said.

"Why is it naive? Why isn't it brilliant? We've got something he wants badly. We've got leverage. Why can't we use it to catch him?"

"Stuff like that only happens in the movies, Charlie." Rick's expression told him to get real.

Charlie burned with frustration. "Why? Because it's what we all want so badly? Dreams only come true in make-believe, is that what you're saying?"

"Reality isn't always pretty," Hunt said.

"Then why do the three of you come to work every day if nothing you do will make a difference?"

The cops looked chagrined and resigned.

Juliana took a deep breath. "I'll help you, Charlie." He looked at her in awe, hope rising. She looked frightened but resolved. "I'll go with you to California. Hell, give me a photo of this drug lord and I'll take you to him."

"Juliana," Montoya scolded. Rick chimed in, too.

"If one person can make a difference," she said, "then two should be able to make twice the difference. And I have a gift." She rose and looked at Charlie. "I'll need things from my apartment. We can make airline reservations from there."

"You can't go," Montoya said. "It's too dangerous. You should be in protective custody."

"I've been in protective custody since I was sixteen. No more. Charlie needs me." Her eyes glittered with challenge. "C'mon, Charlie. Without a Miranda they're screwed and they know it." She picked up his jacket and held it out to him. He stepped to her side and took it.

"I need my bags," he said.

"My dad will get them." She glared into the mirror. "Won't you, Dad?" She turned back to Charlie. "You ready?"

He looked at the detectives. "I would have liked your help. A soldier doesn't like to go into battle alone."

"Especially against overwhelming odds," Juliana added.

Charlie couldn't help smiling at her. "We could make a mint in Vegas betting on those odds. Remind me to call an odds maker I know from the airport." They headed for the door.

A chair screeched. "Charlie, don't be stupid," Rick said.

Charlie turned and faced his brother. "This is the clearest my thinking has been in years. Tell Mom I'm sorry I couldn't stay."

Juliana pushed open the door, and Charlie followed her out. Her father met them in the hall. "This is crazy. I forbid you to go."

"It's the right thing to do," Juliana said. "And I'm going. I'm done allowing you to protect me. We need a ride to my place."

Her father looked from her mulish face to Charlie's set one. His shoulders drooped. "I'll get you released."

Charlie felt like a phoenix rising from the ashes. Yes, they were going into a dangerous situation. But he'd have Juliana at his side like old times. Hot damn.

• • •

They had their plane reservations. Charlie would drive them to the airport so he could return his rental car. Juliana packed, and she and Charlie changed clothes. They'd altered their appearance as much as they could. Juliana's hair was tucked into a French braid. Charlie had his hair slicked back and sported a mustache and goatee. They both knew the danger they'd be in from the time they arrived at the airport until they got past the security barriers if Montgomery had regained consciousness.

Charlie touched her cheek. "Juliana, you'd be safer here."

"I'm going with you."

He closed his eyes then opened them. He lifted his bag. "Ready?"

Juliana looked around her homey apartment, at the colored pots she loved. She lived and worked here. It was safe, but she was just learning it was a prison, and she'd allowed it to happen. Her world had shrunken in so many ways since she'd lost Charlie. If she'd been stronger, she could have broken free. But she hadn't. Because *he* hadn't been here.

Things would be different when she returned. *She* would be different. She was going to live with Charlie until this was over. They would share their lives—and their bodies—for as long as it took. She'd help him achieve his dream and build new ones of her own.

She drew in a breath and set her shoulders. "I'm ready." She'd be with Charlie. She'd followed him into adventure and excitement through childhood and adolescence, and he'd kept her safe. Now she would follow him once more, only this time, she'd do everything she could to keep him safe.

But when they exited her apartment, they found Rick Ziffkin instead of her father. Juliana braced for trouble.

Charlie stopped on the stairs. "Rick."

Rick straightened from where he leaned against a tan sedan. "I'm driving you to the airport. If I can't stop you from this insanity, I'll at least make sure you're safe." He held up his hand to forestall whatever Charlie was going to say. "I know someone in the DEA from a case I worked last month. I called him. A DEA agent named David Fuentes will meet your flight in California."

Charlie's grip on her wrist relaxed, and he continued down the stairs. "Thanks, Rick."

"They're not guaranteeing anything beyond hearing you out," Rick cautioned.

"I'll do this on my own if I have to." Charlie glanced at Juliana. "Juliana and I will. But we'd have a better chance of success with their help."

Rick strode forward and took a bag from each of them. "Do you have bandages to take care of that arm?"

They followed him to the car. "Yeah. Juliana bought some last night."

"Did you get blood in the car?" Rick asked in a sharp voice. "Did you use your rental?"

"Yeah," Charlie admitted.

"I'll get it cleaned before I take it back to the rental agency. Maybe keep it another day. Give me the keys."

Charlie dug in his pocket and handed over the keys. "Thanks. I didn't think about that. It's Enterprise. It's the dark gray one over there."

Rick pocketed them. "You haven't been a P.I. long. Do you do it part time?" He opened the trunk.

Charlie handed Rick his garment bag. "I'm a full-time P.I. I don't have any other job."

"Until you get bored and go back to acting." Rick loaded Juliana's bag and slammed the trunk.

"That's not going to happen. I told you I gave up acting."

Rick scoffed. "When?"

"After Billy died."

"I don't believe it."

Charlie shrugged. "Whatever." He opened the back door for Juliana. She saw the pain in his eyes and looked from him to his brother.

"Talk to him," she whispered.

"I told you they can't accept it. I need this sting to show my family I really am different."

She gripped his wrist. "If something happens to you, to me—"

"Nothing's going to happen."

"There are no guarantees in life. We both know that people die unexpectedly every day. You should make peace with your brother. Sit in the front with him."

"It won't do any good."

"Please."

He sighed. She slid into the back seat, and he closed the door. At least she'd hugged her father and told him she loved him. She knew he didn't understand any more than Charlie's brother did.

Charlie and Rick slid into the front seats. Rick glanced at her. She gave him an encouraging smile. He started the car and headed for the airport.

"I was wasting my life out there, Rick," Charlie began.

Rick glanced over at him. "What do you mean? You always wanted to be an actor."

"I barely made a living. I had to work other jobs to make ends meet. I've been living in apartments for twelve years."

"You're waiting for your big break. And I live in an apartment. Lots of people do."

"I'm at the same place as thousands of eighteen-year-olds who've just arrived in Hollywood. My big break's not coming."

"You got discouraged, I understand. But you can't give up your dream."

"It's done. When Billy died I re-examined my life. I'll never be smart like him or cure cancer like he might have, but I can do more than sell toothpaste."

"Charlie, do you think you're dumb because you're an actor and not a biochemist?"

"I didn't even go to college."

"You still can. They have plenty of schools out there in California."

"You don't understand. I like what I'm doing now. I've made a difference to a few of my clients. I never made a difference before."

Rick was silent for the rest of the trip. Charlie hadn't spoken with the despair he'd used to discuss his life choice with Juliana, but sincerity resonated in his voice. She hoped Rick heard it, too.

Rick pulled up to the terminal. "I'll make sure you get inside, then go park the car."

He flashed his badge, which got a nod from security. He guarded them while they checked their bags, his eyes scanning the area around them. Then he walked them to the door.

"I'll be back as soon as I park the car."

"Right." Charlie tugged her into the air-conditioned building. They walked straight to the security line. Juliana kept hold of his hand while she surveyed the crowd.

"Don't be nervous." He kissed her temple. "You'll attract attention."

"They could be here waiting."

"Then relax so you don't stand out. Think about spending the next few days at my place. No interruptions. We don't have to get out of bed if we don't want to. You can live out all your fantasies on my body."

"*All* of them? I have a lot."

"Even the kinky ones. I'll be your willing sex slave."

Her lower body clenched in anticipation. "We got the tape back from the cops."

"Oh, you're naughty."

"Not yet, but I'm going to be."

"I can't wait."

By the time it was their turn to enter the metal detectors, Rick rejoined them. He waited with them for their flight, which gave him and Charlie more time to talk. Juliana noticed Rick's interest in her relationship with Charlie. The cop's eyes noted every touch, caress, kiss, and intimacy. They catalogued how Charlie and Juliana held hands, Charlie's use of her nickname, and how they looked at one another. Like many cops, including her father, Rick had learned to control his face, so she wasn't sure how he felt about her and Charlie.

When their flight was called, Rick walked them to the gate. "Keep your eyes and ears open, both of you. This isn't a game."

"We know," Charlie assured him.

Rick hugged him. "I don't want to get a phone call saying I've lost another brother. I love you, Charlie."

"I'll be careful. I love you, too."

"Watch your back."

Billy Ziffkin had been stabbed in the back.

Rick let go of his brother and held his arms open for Juliana. She went into them, and he hugged her tight. "Take care of Charlie," he whispered.

"I will."

"I'm glad he has you." He released her.

She took Charlie's offered hand, and they walked down the jet way toward their chance to prove themselves to their families. Five and a half hours later they entered the baggage claim area at LAX. A Latino man held a cardboard sign that read "Ziffkin."

"I'm Ziffkin," Charlie said.

"Fuentes, DEA." The man showed them his I.D., then waited while they collected their luggage. "Where can I take you?"

"To Jordan Hessler's house preferably, but I live in Van Nuys," Charlie replied. "Is your office closer?"

"Van Nuys it is. My partner will bring the car around. Then we can talk." He led them toward the doors. "Nobody followed you?"

"Not that we saw. My brother, who's with the Miami P.D., waited with us at the terminal."

"He gave me a summary of what's going on. Nobody knew who you were when you retrieved this relic?"

"I don't think Montgomery's men got either of our license plates. But if they find out who Jordan Hessler hired, they'll know who I am."

"Hmm, loose end."

"Or if they bribe the car rental agents to divulge any cars rented by Californians in the past week."

"That's a lot of leads. And that's assuming they know you're from California." Fuentes scanned outside, then led them through the sliding doors into the cool California evening that made Juliana shiver after the hot Miami afternoon.

A big dark sedan pulled up driven by a man with his brown hair in a ponytail.

"Our ride," Fuentes said.

They stuffed the luggage in the truck and piled into the car.

The driver showed his I.D. "Kurt Steiger, DEA. Where to?"

Charlie told him and the car sped away from the curb.

Fuentes turned around to face them. "So you made an enemy in Miami. Montgomery's going to be gunning for somebody now that he's awake."

CHAPTER 17

"Montgomery's awake?" Charlie repeated. God, he'd hoped for more time. Where was a coma when you needed one? "Did his shooting make the national news?"

"No," Fuentes replied. "Your brother called to tell me."

Well, that was something. "But you think he'll be gunning for me?"

"If he learns who you are. The two drug dealers he didn't kill are probably pretty pissed, too."

"Yeah." Charlie hadn't thought of that at the time.

Fuentes echoed Charlie's thought. "What were you thinking, to steal from Dalton Montgomery like that?"

Charlie shrugged. "I was just doing my job."

"Your brother told me your sting idea. We'd have to catch Jordan Hessler breaking the law, and I can't see him doing that when you return the stolen relic to him."

Charlie burned with frustration. "But he supplies drugs. That's against the law."

"We'll be able to build a case against him after he gets a drug pipeline with the relic."

"But that'll be too late. While we've got the sculpture is the time to use it to catch all the crooks we can."

"You obviously don't understand how law enforcement works. We need evidence of wrongdoing."

"Tell me what you need, and I can help you get it."

Fuentes shook his head. "Turn the relic over to Hessler and get the hell out of Dodge. We'll get a wiretap on his phone and e-mail and document the exchange of the relic for the drug pipeline. When he starts dealing, we'll have him."

"Just give him the keys to the kingdom," Charlie said, unable to contain his bitterness.

"Hey, it'll be a big bust when it finally goes down," Steiger said. "You can be proud of making us aware of it."

"It's a waste of a perfect opportunity," Charlie disagreed. "I'd be better off putting the relic in a safety deposit box for the remainder of my life. At least that would accomplish something."

"But your way Hessler goes free. Our way he doesn't," Fuentes said.

"My way, a really bad guy doesn't get what he wants." Charlie looked at Juliana. In the passing streetlights her wide eyes showed her empathy. Damn it, he'd liked the idea she'd get to witness him play the hero. "Well, I guess I can wait to see Hessler until tomorrow then."

"You want us to hold the relic for safekeeping?" Steiger offered. "We can lock it up with the drugs in the police evidence locker."

Charlie felt a chill. He didn't know these agents—they could be dirty, or the sculpture could tempt them beyond resistance. If he gave them the sculpture, they might trade it and he'd lose any opportunity he had to use it against criminals.

"I don't have it with me," Charlie lied. Juliana jerked against his side.

"What?" Fuentes's head snapped around. "I thought this was all about stinging Hessler with the relic."

Charlie felt Juliana's stare burning into him. "I couldn't have gotten it through airport security. God, that would have been a nightmare, sprawled facedown on the floor with a dozen guns pointed at me. I would have been locked up for months trying to assure somebody I wasn't a terrorist."

"Then what did you do with it?" Steiger asked.

"I shipped it. What else?"

"Pretty smart." Fuentes's smile gleamed in the streetlights. "It gets the relic out from under Montgomery's nose."

"Yeah, I thought so. So, can you wire me for sound tomorrow when I go see Hessler? You never know what he might admit. And if you've got a bug you can spare, I'll plant it for you."

Fuentes looked at Steiger before replying. "We'll see what we can do. Give me your cell number and I'll call you tomorrow." He held out a business card and Charlie took it. "That's how you can contact me."

The DEA agents dropped Charlie and Juliana at his apartment in Van Nuys.

"Home sweet home." Charlie tried to envision the two-story converted single-family home from Juliana's point of view. The style was modern, its slanted rooflines, skylights, and high windows being the closest he could come to his native Miami architecture. He liked the cedar shingles and the plentiful landscaping. A few of the deciduous shrubs lent a delightful piney tang to freshen the heavy LA air.

"I thought you lived in an apartment," Juliana said.

"I do. Mine is on the right. The owners converted the house into a twinplex about ten years ago."

Charlie unlocked his door trying to remember if he'd left anything lying on the floor. He opened the door, turned on the light, and waved her inside.

Juliana looked around with curious brown eyes. "It's bigger than I thought."

"The cathedral ceilings make the space deceptive. That's why I chose it." He closed and locked the door. She was here. He'd wished for this day, but never thought it would happen.

She wandered from his living room into his small kitchen and dining room. "No flower pots."

"Sorry, no room."

"I noticed every available space is filled with books and DVDs."

"My former craft."

"You're very neat." Juliana turned to face him. "You weren't that way at my place."

"I only thought of one thing at your place."

She raised her eyebrows. "And you don't think of it here?"

"Hell, yes, I do. My God, you're living with me for who knows how long. But this is the first time you've seen my life here. I'm kind of … nervous."

Juliana moved close to him and walked her fingers up his arm. His fingers curled in response. "You, nervous?"

"Yeah." He smiled at her. "I want to make a good impression."

"You don't need to impress me, Charlie. 'You had me at hello,'" she quoted.

Charlie smiled even wider. "Would you like to see the bedroom?"

"See. Do. Lead on."

He took her hand and pulled her up the stairs to his bedroom. He had made the bed, thank God. The twelve-foot wall, topped by a row of windows, made a dramatic backdrop for the double bed and sunset-patterned comforter. He wished now for a king-sized bed. Another row of windows filled the side wall and looked out onto a sloping roof and grassy back yard.

"Women must be impressed by this room," Juliana murmured as she took in the room's details.

Charlie turned Juliana to face him. "No woman has ever been here. I moved here after Billy died."

"Don't your lovers wonder why you won't take them home?"

"Juliana, I haven't been interested in sex since Billy died. Not until I saw you in that hooker get-up. And then I could hardly think of anything else."

Juliana frowned. "You haven't made love for two years? But you're so good at it. You don't seem out of practice."

"You're mistaking desperate desire for experience."

She licked her lips. "Well, that explains the last few days then." Her smile spread across her face like the sun rising. His heart lifted.

"I think we need to divest you of clothes and the sculpture so we can get busy christening this bed."

"And the rest of the apartment," he added, hope rising as well as his cock.

"One room at a time. Starting here." Juliana reached for the large chambray shirt he had on over his T-shirt.

Charlie allowed her to remove it. She tossed it to the floor. Next they pulled his shirt over his head, uncovering the sculpture and all the rows of black electrical tape.

She pursed her lips and found one of the ends on the bottom row. Tugging, the tape came off as soundlessly as it had gone on. It pulled on his skin but didn't hurt. She gave him the strip to hold and attacked the next row. His flesh itched where the tape had been and he noticed it left a red welt on his body. He held the sculpture while she removed the final rows of tape.

"Ow!" He'd tried to prepare himself to lose a few chest hairs from the last row, but that clump had hurt.

"Sorry."

"It's okay. At least I didn't have more."

When the sculpture was free, he handed it to her so he could rub at what appeared to be a bruise. Damn those Miami narcs.

"This thing has a bloody history," Juliana breathed, frowning.

"What do you mean?"

"I mean a lot of people died getting this sculpture, stealing it, hiding it."

"You can see it?"

She nodded, staring at the sculpture. "It contains echoes, powerful echoes. It's old."

"Then it really is a relic?"

"Yes. So many faces. Such greed. Such evil. I feel touches of good, but they don't last long. A period of darkness that lasted until recently, when it must have been found. Charlie, every time someone evil had it in their hands, they believed it held power."

"And that's why the drug lord wants it? Because he believes what those others believed?"

"It must be."

"Does it contain power?" Charlie couldn't believe he'd asked that question.

"No. The power was in what the people who held it believed. And evil men can become very powerful with evil deeds."

Charlie inhaled a breath to clear his head. "They believed, therefore they were?"

"Maybe." Juliana shuddered and handed the sculpture back to him. "Too much blood. Too much death."

He didn't question her. He understood nothing about her psychic power beyond that she could find objects from photos. He laid the sculpture on his nightstand. For some reason, he didn't want it far from the bed.

Juliana rubbed her arms. He touched her and felt her chill.

"C'mon, let's take a shower. I need you to scrub this sticky stuff off me." He herded her into the bathroom.

With eager hands, Juliana stripped off his khaki pants and underwear. He pulled off her knit top and jeans skirt. He took a moment to admire her matching peach underwear set. She looked delectable. He ran a caressing hand over her breasts, which made her nipples peak. She reached behind her and unhooked her bra, drawing it off to reveal those mouth-watering globes. He got both hands on them while she shimmied out of her underwear.

"Charlie," she protested in a breathy voice.

Then her hands reached between his legs and, oh, God, that felt good. His cock responded to her caresses by growing firm and thick. He barely had enough brain cells north of the border to turn on the shower and adjust the temperature.

"Umm," he murmured into her hair. He nipped her ear.

Juliana made her own relishing noises. She had nimble, eager fingers. He thrust into her hands. Her nipples were tight points between his fingers. He was panting. Being with her always did this to him.

"Into the shower," he managed.

They shared the soap, kissing while their mingled fingers lathered. Then she slid her eager hands over his chest scrubbing at the tape marks. His soapy hands slid over her breasts, over the tight nipples. Her breath hitched. She lifted her lips for a kiss, and he complied.

As much as he desired to fill her and make urgent love to her, he also wanted to caress and kiss her all over, and have her do the same to him. He wanted to worship her in his home and let her know she was more than a sexual vessel here in California.

Juliana turned him to scrub at the stickiness on his back. He used the opportunity to take a deep breath and try to control the need he felt only for her. Her scrubbing was practical, necessary, it shouldn't feel sexual at all. Until her hands slid down to caress his butt. There her caresses were anything but practical. His cock throbbed with need.

As though she knew how her touch affected him, her hands left his buttocks. He sighed with relief and regret. But then they slid around his hips to grip his cock. She pressed her warm, soft body against his back as she caressed him. Charlie threw back his head and gritted his teeth. Despite his iron control, his hips thrust, driving his cock through her soapy fingers.

"That feels so good," he groaned.

"Yes, it does." She caressed his length. "I love your cock, how silky and strong it feels, how it feels when your first thrust enters me, how it feels as you move inside me."

"You're killing me."

Her grip tightened as she stroked back and forth. "How it feels when you come."

"Don't." His hands gripped hers on his cock. "I want to be inside you when I come."

He gentled her grip and her movements and then lifted her hands away, turning in her embrace. He grabbed the soap and lathered his hands. Hers joined his on the soap. He lowered his head to give her a long, languid kiss. Their tongues touched, stroked. Her hands massaged his chest. He broke the kiss at last and held her away from him so he could slip a hand between her soft thighs.

He found the tight bud of her clit. As he stroked, she inhaled. He soaped her channel next, opening her body for the loving to come. Her hips thrust forward.

When no more soap remained, he undid Juliana's French braid and massaged shampoo into her hair. She hummed her appreciation. Quickly he washed his own hair. Then he turned off the water and dropped to his knees in front of her.

Charlie looked up at her as water drops slid down her body over her full breasts, slender abdomen, and feminine hips, all the places he wanted to lick. With her hair wet, she looked like a water nymph here to share sexual delights with him.

"You're beautiful."

Her eyes were dark with desire. "So are you."

"Lean down."

She did and he took her breast into his mouth to lick off the drops of water. Her breathing increased as he paid tribute to her wonderful nipple, licking it as he knew she liked. When that breast was fully loved, he took the other one into his mouth. Juliana slid her hands into his wet hair and gripped his head in place. She needn't fear he was leaving this feast.

He bit gently on her nipple. She made appreciative sounds deep in her throat. With reluctance he let her breast slide from his mouth. She had other delights he needed to explore. He sucked moisture from her abdomen, kissing her hickey, probing her naval, and then licked south.

He dipped his head between her legs to lick her clit. She gasped. He laved the sensitive nubbin, loving the jerks her body made in response. Then he began to suck. She rewarded him with groans that shortened as she came in his mouth. Her knees gave out.

Charlie opened the shower door and laid Juliana on the bath mat. He grabbed a condom from his pants pocket and sheathed himself. She watched with a languid gaze. He knelt, spreading her legs, and licked her channel. He teased her pussy, tasting her sweet essence, until he brought her to the peak once more, and she came again.

As she moaned, he mounted her and thrust into her body. Her body gripped his, the rhythmic clamping of her orgasm caressing him even as he thrust. She cried out, her hips lifting to take him deep inside her. Charlie strained to hold back his orgasm. He wanted to experience all the wonders of Juliana's body.

With rough, urgent thrusts he plumbed her depths. Juliana was just as urgent, even though she'd come twice already. He gripped her bottom and pulled her into a deep thrust, coming hard inside her. He held her to him. How had they waited this many hours to be joined like this? He ground his body into hers.

Charlie needed to let Juliana know she should have been here with him all along. He had more than a decade of emptiness to make up for.

They collapsed to the floor. He kissed the side of her face. "Welcome to your home away from home. I'm glad you came."

"So am I. I'm also glad I'm here."

"Naughty." He bit her neck.

"Not yet, but I will be later."

"Juliana … " He stumbled over the magnitude of what he felt for her.

"What?"

"I could do this with you forever and never grow tired of doing it."

"I feel the same."

"Why is it only with you?" he murmured.

"Because we were meant to be together?"

"We *are* a perfect fit." He was still hard. He wanted her again, but he wanted to let her have her way with him first. He withdrew slowly. Then he kissed her hard. If only he could keep her. If only he deserved a woman like her.

Juliana reached between his legs and felt his cock. "Ready to go again I see. What room do you want to christen next?"

CHAPTER 18

"Do I get to go with you to meet Jordan Hessler?" Juliana asked when Charlie hung up the phone.

Charlie wrapped an arm around her waist and tugged her into his lap. "I think he'll speak more freely if I'm alone. We want him to give himself away."

"I know, but I don't want you to face him alone."

Charlie kissed her. "You're a good woman."

Juliana laced her arms around his neck. "I'm good for you. You should keep me around."

He smiled. "I wish I could, but what would your father say?"

"He's not my spokesman. What would *I* say?"

"You'd say call those DEA agents and set everything up."

Juliana hid her disappointment. Charlie avoided any talk of commitment. Now that he knew there wasn't going to be a sting, he'd lost some of his animation. It had meant something to him, represented something to him. She knew what it had meant to her. She wished with all her heart he could do the sting, because when he'd thought he was going to conquer villains, he'd wanted her by his side.

He wanted her now, desperately, with a palpable need, but he held back. Not his body, God, no. Not his neediness. He couldn't stop touching her, mating with her. It was so much more than sex between them. He tried to brand her, possess her, consume her, make them one. But then he'd retreat.

She didn't understand. He wanted that unity so badly, but he pulled back afterward. And then he sought it with her again. She ached from the number of times they'd made love last night. And that last time had taken them nearly an hour to come.

Juliana laid her head on his shoulder. He nuzzled her face and lifted the phone again. His voice rumbled through her body as he asked for Agent Fuentes. She accepted his kiss.

"Agent Fuentes, it's Charlie Ziffkin. I'm set to meet Jordan Hessler at four today."

He listened. She could faintly hear a man's voice.

"Sure. We'll look for you at three." Then he hung up.

"We have three hours. What would you like to do in that time?" Charlie waggled his eyebrows. His erection was growing under her bottom.

"As much as I'd like to rip your pants off and bury you deep inside me, I'm hungry and you don't have much to eat in the house."

He nuzzled beneath her ear. "I could be persuaded to feed your appetite if you feed mine."

Juliana pulled away from his wicked lips. "You should be sated. I lost track of the times I fed yours."

Charlie tried to tug her back to him. "I'll never be sated. How about a quickie before we find food?"

"Charlie, once you get my clothes off we're not going to stop until the DEA agents knock on the door." His erection was a hard insistence now.

"Party pooper. It's been hours since we made love."

"We were asleep," Juliana pointed out. "Exhausted. Worn out."

"I've got my second wind."

"Food. Then I swear you can do whatever you want."

His eyebrows shot up. "Anything?"

Juliana felt her eyes widen. What did he want to do that they hadn't tried already? She was intrigued. He'd lived in California for more than a decade. They were on the cutting edge out here. He'd probably learned a lot of sexual tricks before he became a born-again virgin.

"Yes. You can do anything."

The aphrodisiac massage oils Charlie bought at a sex shop on the way back from the fast food restaurant had the unfortunate side effect of giving them an itch they couldn't scratch. They were still trying to appease their sexual hunger when the DEA agents arrived.

"Oh, God, they're here," Charlie groaned. The sound vibrated across her clit.

"Why didn't you tell me that stuff lasted for hours? Right there. Please. Oh, Charlie." She gripped his butt as he brought her close to climax with his plundering tongue.

The doorbell pealed again. He lifted his head and she squawked her protest. She was so close.

"We have to do this." Charlie climbed off the bed. He pulled up his jeans over his thick erection.

"You have to do *me*. You did this to me!"

"I'll let them in. Or send them away." He ran a distracted hand through his wild waves, threw on his shirt without buttoning it, and headed out of the bedroom.

Juliana should never have promised him anything. She shouldn't have agreed to the aphrodisiac. She smiled despite her burning clitoris and aching pussy. They'd had a really good time.

She heard male voices and then Charlie was back. He closed the bedroom door, dropped his jeans and shirt, and climbed onto the bed. He mounted her, entering her hard.

"Charlie," she protested. "They're downstairs!"

"I said we had an aphrodisiac mishap. They gave me fifteen minutes." He grunted quietly as he thrust.

Juliana gritted her teeth and ground herself into him. "Mishap."

His smile flashed again. "Be thankful the bed doesn't squeak."

They strained and twisted and pressed together until they came.

"I'm still horny," Juliana complained as she gripped him to her.

"Tough. Welcome to my life," Charlie said. "Time's up."

They dressed, hid the sculpture, and went to meet the agents. Juliana's face felt as hot as her clit. She could barely stand still while they taped a mike to Charlie's bare chest.

"Tape," Charlie grumbled.

"It should only hurt a little coming off," Agent Fuentes said.

Charlie snorted.

"What's this bruise and red abrasion?" the agent asked.

"The Miami narcs got a little rough when I wouldn't let them arrest me."

Fuentes lifted both brows. "I haven't heard that story."

"I don't need further humiliation right now," Charlie responded, which made the agents smile.

Charlie led the way to Hessler's mansion on Coldwater Canyon Drive north of Beverly Hills. It was a modern sprawling structure made of lots of glass, one of many houses jutting out on the hillside.

Juliana rode with the DEA agents in their plain white van. They drove on a little way past Hessler's driveway before stopping. Then Fuentes and Steiger climbed out and entered the back of the van, where the electronic surveillance equipment was, and where Juliana sat on the floor. They donned headsets and gave her one.

A man's smooth baritone spoke clearly. "Charlie, glad you're back. Come into my office so we can talk."

Traffic sounds ceased as Charlie moved indoors. Hessler asked, "How was your trip?"

"The flight out was uneventful, but I brought my high school girlfriend back with me. We reconnected after all these years. I've got you to thank for that."

"Glad to hear it. Have a seat." A door closed. "So where's my sculpture?"

Cloth rubbed against the microphone as Charlie sat. "I shipped it. It'll be here tomorrow morning. I didn't want to take it on the plane."

"You know how important it is for me to get it back." Hessler sounded a little impatient.

"I know what you told me. You should have warned me there'd be drug dealers after it and it would be dangerous."

"I didn't know about that." Hessler sounded shocked.

"Cut the crap," Charlie snapped. "I hear rumors. I know actors get drugs at your parties."

A chair creaked. "I can't help what my guests give each other."

"Right, you don't provide any of it, do you?"

"Of course not. Drugs are illegal."

Charlie snorted. "I charge extra for dangerous assignments."

The chair squeaked again. "I'll pay the additional when you bring me the sculpture."

"Fine." Rustling cloth indicated Charlie was moving. "Mr. Hessler, why did you hire me? You could have hired a big name." The sound came from two difference sources, so Charlie must have planted the bug.

"You needed the money. And I thought you'd be discreet. You don't hang out much with the acting crowd any more I hear."

"No, not anymore."

"You'll call me as soon as the sculpture arrives?"

"First thing," Charlie agreed.

"Great." Hessler's voice moved closer. "I'll see you out."

The two men were silent as they walked to the door. The door opened. "I'll expect your call," Hessler said. The door closed.

Back in the van, Fuentes sighed. "Nothing."

"You warned him," Steiger said.

Juliana ached for Charlie, knowing he'd wanted the sting so badly. She couldn't imagine him handing over the sculpture to Hessler tomorrow. It was going to haunt him.

She watched through the back window as Charlie drove his car back down the way they'd come.

Through her headphones Juliana heard Hessler sigh as he sank into a chair in his office. A drawer opened. Then there was a pause, followed by, "It's Jordan Hessler. I need to speak to Mr. Gutierrez."

Agents Fuentes and Steiger exchanged a wide-eyed, excited look.

"Miguel," Hessler dropped into Spanish, which Juliana spoke fluently. It appeared the DEA agents did as well. "My agent has recovered the item. How do you wish to proceed? The day after tomorrow? And my first shipment? The sixteenth. Good. You can count on me, Mr. Gutierrez. *Adios*."

"Jesus Christ," Fuentes exclaimed, pulling off his headphones. "We have to find out how the drugs are coming in."

Steiger removed his own headphones. "I think we have enough to get a wire tap." His grin nearly split his face.

Juliana handed her headphones to Fuentes. "Surely the man coming to pick up the sculpture knows the details. Grab him and make him talk."

"We can't grab him without just cause," Fuentes explained, as to a child.

"Besides," Steiger added, "we can't do anything to tip off Gutierrez. We won't interfere with the courier."

"You'd rather allow the drugs into the country," Juliana accused.

"It allows us to arrest people," Fuentes explained. "It also allows us to try to get a man inside and work back to Gutierrez."

"That takes years, years of drugs flooding the country, killing our citizens and our cops, and ruining millions of lives."

"We don't create the need for drugs," Steiger snapped.

"No, you just ride the supply chain. Take me down the road to Charlie. He should hear this."

The agents scowled, then slid into the front to drive down to the pre-arranged rendezvous point. Charlie's black sedan sat at the gas station. Fuentes signaled him over. The back door opened and he stepped in, followed by Fuentes. Charlie reached for her hand

and she gripped his. He sat in the chair beside her and leaned down to give her a quick kiss. She felt his tension.

"Did you get anything you can use to arrest Hessler?" Charlie asked.

"No. That only happens on TV or in the movies. But listen to this." Fuentes gave Charlie a set of headphones and played back the recording of Hessler's phone call.

Charlie's face lit up. "We've got 'em! You can arrest Hessler picking up his drugs and this guy coming in can lead you right back to Gutierrez."

"We're not going to be able to trail Gutierrez's representative without tipping him off and blowing a bust. We won't risk that."

"You're just going to let Gutierrez get away? He's the prize, not Hessler."

"We have to work within the law. Gutierrez doesn't."

"Damn!" Charlie jerked off the headphones.

Juliana touched his thigh. He covered her hand with his and looked at her with pain-filled eyes. She ached for him. He'd said he wanted to make a difference, but he couldn't.

He squeezed her hand. "Let's go home."

"Yes," she agreed with alacrity.

Charlie climbed out of the van and helped her down. Agent Fuentes followed them out and shut the door. He held out his hand and Charlie shook it.

"You did good planting the bug. It gave us a chance for a bust. It was a good day."

"Sure."

"Call us when the package arrives."

"Yeah."

Charlie took her hand and they walked to his car. The white van headed for the road with a wave from Fuentes.

Charlie stood a minute watching it drive away. "There must be something we can do to catch Gutierrez. They may have to work within the law, but I don't."

CHAPTER 19

Charlie jerked awake, his heart pounding. He stilled, listening for whatever had woken him. Juliana slept tucked against his body. Her soft breaths weren't the sound he'd heard.

There. A soft thud. He covered Juliana's mouth with his hand and placed his lips against her ear. "Jules, wake up." He shook her with his other hand. "Jules."

She made a muffled sound against his hand. "Jules, someone's downstairs."

Her eyes snapped open. In the faint moonlight they were wide with fear.

"I'm going downstairs." He let go of her.

Juliana grabbed his arm. "No! It's too dangerous." Her whisper throbbed with fear.

"I have to. If anything happens, climb out the window. You can slide down close to the ground and jump. Take the sculpture. Run. Get on the next plane home to your father."

"No. Not without you."

"Jules, I have to do this."

He snatched his blue jeans from the floor and tugged them on. Juliana slid out of bed. Grabbing the baseball bat he kept stashed next to the bedroom door, he slipped out into the short hallway. His heart pounded hard as he crept down the stairs, avoiding the places that creaked. His palms felt sweaty on the bat. Whoever was downstairs wasn't getting to Juliana. He'd meant it when he said he'd die to protect her. But he hoped he wouldn't have to do that.

A dark silhouette appeared at the bottom of the stairs. Charlie's heart jumped into his throat. The figure raised something that gleamed. A gun! Charlie's launched himself toward the man. He heard a whooshing sound and felt a hot brand slice his side.

He hit the man with all his weight. They tumbled on the ground together, and bumped into something that grunted. A second man! Charlie scrambled off the first man and came up swinging toward the second intruder. The bat connected with a satisfying thud. The man yowled in pain and stumbled back.

The shooter grabbed Charlie from behind, pinning his arms to his sides. Charlie twisted, trying to throw him off. They careened into a bookshelf. Plastic DVD cases made a clattering ruckus as they flew in all directions. Books thumped to the floor.

Charlie and the shooter flung each other one way and then another, running into the wall. But the man clung like a burr. Suddenly, a dark shadow rose in front of Charlie. The second intruder. Charlie rammed the intruder in the abdomen with the bat. The man made a strangled inhalation and dropped to the floor.

Pain tore through Charlie's wounded arm. The son of a bitch shooter had ripped the stitches open. Charlie felt wetness as the wound bled. If he didn't break free soon this bastard would wear him down. Had Juliana escaped yet? He couldn't hear anything from upstairs. He slammed the shooter into the kitchen counter. The man's hold slipped on the blood. Charlie spun free, swinging the bat with all his might. There was a sickening crack and the shooter crumpled.

The other intruder was rising from the floor. There was the glint of metal in his hand. Charlie swung the bat and connected with his arm and a metal clack told Charlie he'd knocked the gun away.

The intruder stumbled away toward the front door. Charlie chased him, but slipped on a DVD and slid into the wall with a thud. Pain slammed into his wounded arm, and he saw stars.

When his head cleared, the front door stood open and empty. Juliana! He rushed for the stairs only to be blinded by the lights in the stairwell. Juliana stood there with his pocketknife extended threateningly, wearing only his T-shirt.

"Juliana." Relief crashed over him.

"Charlie, you're hurt!"

"Grab my bag, my wallet, and the sculpture. We've got to get out of here."

She looked like she wanted to ask questions. But she spun around and ran for the bedroom.

Charlie collected the intruders' guns and a set of car keys from his kitchen cabinet. His apartment was a mess. The bookshelf leaned drunkenly. Books and DVDs were scattered over the floor. Blood stained the walls and carpet.

The shooter lay sprawled on the kitchen floor. A dark stain pooled by his head. When Charlie crouched beside him, sharp pain stabbed his side. He looked down to find the bullet had grazed him, but not penetrated. There was no time to tend to his wound. He rifled the man's pockets and found a wallet, which he opened and held up to the light.

Miami, Florida. Son of a bitch. Montgomery's men.

They could only have gotten his address from Hessler. Charlie was going to pay that bastard a visit and wring the truth out of him. It was … he looked at the clock on the kitchen stove and saw it was four-twenty in the morning. They'd drag Hessler out of bed. Charlie gripped the bat. Maybe they'd use a little persuasion.

"Oh, my God!" Juliana exclaimed beside him, nearly scaring the crap out of him. She pulled the wallet toward her. "Montgomery."

"Yeah."

"Is he dead?"

"I was afraid to check, and I don't really want to know. We have to go. The other one got away but he might come back."

She'd changed into her own clothes. Both their bags stood behind her.

"Got everything?" he asked.

"Yes and I brought you clothes and shoes."

"Let's go. Turn off the light."

Juliana retreated to the stairwell and did as he asked. Then she rejoined him. "What about your wounds?"

Charlie grabbed some kitchen towels, pressed them against his side, and herded her out the front door.

When she turned toward his car, he whispered, "This way."

She followed him to his neighbor's old Ford Taurus. He opened the trunk and Juliana piled in her bag.

But when he headed for the driver's side, she stopped him. "I'll drive."

She placed his bag in the back seat and slid behind the wheel. With a grateful sigh he sank into the passenger's seat.

The Taurus started with a sputter. "Whose car?"

"My neighbor. He's on location in Canada for six weeks."

"Where to?" Her voice quavered a bit.

"To Hessler's house. We're gonna get answers from that bastard."

• • •

They weren't going to get any answers from Jordan Hessler. He lay in a pool of blood on his living room carpet. Juliana stared at the small hole that punctured his forehead. His khaki slacks were scarlet at the knees and ankles. His drug dealing days were over.

"They tortured him for the information." Charlie's face was pale.

"How do you know?" Her stomach turned at the sight of all that blood.

He pointed to Hessler's slacks. "Shooting somebody there is painful but not fatal. Pain's a great motivator." Charlie swallowed. "I wonder if he told them about Gutierrez?"

"I don't care. Let's call the police and get out of here." She turned to go.

"Wait."

She stopped.

"Hessler was supposed to meet with Gutierrez's man. Now Hessler's dead but Gutierrez doesn't know it yet. I've got a small window of opportunity."

"For what?" She felt confused.

"For me to play Hessler and meet with Gutierrez."

"He's not meeting with Gutierrez."

"He is now." Charlie held a finger to his lips.

Juliana followed him into Hessler's office. Charlie quietly rifled the desk drawers until he held up a piece of paper with a triumphant smile. He grabbed Hessler's cell phone off the desk, then urged her out the door. When they were far enough from the bug, he showed her the phone number with the initials "M.G." beside it.

After wiping their fingerprints from the door, they retreated to the car.

Juliana didn't start the ignition. "Do we call the DEA?"

"No. I have everything I need to catch Gutierrez. They'd only stop me."

Juliana set her chin.

Charlie pleaded, "Juliana, it's five-thirty. We're going to get caught if we sit here. Let's move."

She started the car and turned onto the road. "You're hurt. You need law enforcement's help."

"This is something the cops can't do. Remember what I said, that a P.I. can go where cops can't, do what they can't do. Their hands are tied. Mine aren't."

"You're a lamb going to the slaughter against Gutierrez. He's the head of a drug cartel."

"I know it's dangerous, but I have to do this. He has to be stopped, and the statue gives me an opportunity no one else will ever have. He's vulnerable because of it, and he probably never will be again. I need to do this for me, and for Billy. Someone like Gutierrez, or maybe even Gutierrez, pumped drugs into New Orleans and into the addict who killed Billy. Nobody ever paid for killing a good man. And I think somebody should.

"But I can't risk you. Head for the airport. I want you on the next plane to Miami. You'll be safe with your father." His voice sounded strained. "You can't know what it means to have somebody in your corner believing in you. You've been there for me. I've missed that."

Juliana's heart felt too big for her chest. She didn't want him risking his life and she sure didn't want him to go on alone. What if he didn't come back? What if he disappeared and she never knew what happened to him or if he'd been killed? She'd regret it for the rest of her life.

"I'll call my father. He can help."

"No. No one knows where we are. Montgomery's thug knows I'm alive. I have to assume Hessler told him the sculpture is coming today, so he'll stick around to try to steal it from me. If we're lucky, the DEA will catch him. Everyone will expect us to remain in town to receive the shipment.

"But if you call your father, he'll call the DEA, and some action of theirs might alert Montgomery's men I'm on the run. And, Jules, I don't know for a fact we can trust the DEA."

She couldn't let Charlie go into danger injured and without backup. Did she really want to make a difference fighting crime? Or was that all talk, like the way she talked about wanting her father to stop smothering her. Here was her chance to really show she didn't want his protection.

She sighed. A cop's daughter on the run. She'd never imagined that scenario. "Where are we running to? I'm coming with you, and nothing you can say will stop me."

There was a long pause before he said, "Mexico. Gutierrez won't come near the States, but he might come to Mexico. The border's not far."

"I've got relatives there." She glanced at him in the luminescence from the dashboard. He looked hopeful. "My father's family is still there—his cousins, aunts, uncles. We travel there every few years for huge get-togethers at a cousin's house just south of the border. I keep my passport up-to-date because of that."

"I wondered. So we're going to your family."

"My second cousin, Felipe Sanchez, lives in Ensenada, ninety minutes from the border. I've never been there. He and his wife, Rosita, have good jobs. They attend every family reunion and have invited my family to stay with them if we're ever in town. They have a spare room now that their son is married."

"Will they let us sleep together? Because if they won't, I don't want to stay there."

Her breath hitched, then her heart galloped. "Don't worry. It's Mexico, not the dark ages. I don't intend to sneak around to make love with you. It will smooth things if I tell them you're my fiancé. Although I have to warn you, Rosita will campaign hard for a wedding."

She concentrated on the road. The sun was rising, the sky lightening. Her body ached with tiredness, but she had to stay alert because with every passing minute more cars filled the road.

"I'm crazy about you, Juliana, you must know that. You make my life worth living. But I don't deserve you. I don't deserve to be happy like that."

Because of Billy. She could fight nearly anything but the ghost of his dead brother. "What about what I want, what I deserve?"

"You deserve better. I have nothing to show for the past dozen years."

"I think you do. You didn't sink into despair or drug addiction. You rebuilt your life into one you can be proud of. You're employed, you pay taxes, and you valued your body enough to hold out for someone you cared about."

"I didn't know that the first night we made love," he said.

"Didn't you?"

Charlie was silent for a few minutes. When he spoke his words were soft. "You were always mine. Even when we were apart and you were letting some other guy take what was mine, you still belonged to me. I wasn't holding out for someone; I was holding out for you."

The road blurred in front of Juliana. "I'd like to spend the rest of my life with you."

"I'd like that, too."

"Then it's settled," she said. "We're engaged."

"Okay." He took several audible breaths. "Listen, we have to stop before we reach the border. I need to get cleaned up and bandaged, and we have some things to hide in case they stop us. I'd better call Gutierrez now. The car noise will help disguise my voice. Don't say anything while I'm on the phone with him."

Charlie dug out Hessler's cell phone and Gutierrez's phone number and dropped into Spanish. "I need to speak to Mr. Gutierrez. It's Jordan Hessler. I know it's early. No, I can't call back. Tell him somebody just tried to kill me for the item he wants."

The whooshing sound of the tires on blacktop filled the car. Tension crept into Juliana's back, neck, and shoulders.

"Miguel, thanks for taking my call. Yes, the item is safe. I have it with me in the car. I'm bloody but alive. I don't know who they were and frankly I'm pretty paranoid right now. I'm changing the plan. I'm on my way to Mexico. I'll be at the border in two hours. I won't be in Los Angeles to meet your man."

Juliana's hands hurt from gripping the wheel tight while praying that Gutierrez believed.

"No, Tijuana is too close to the U.S. I'm driving down to Ensenada. Miguel, last night I had a psychic touch the item."

Charlie paused. "Because I wanted to know why you wanted it so badly. She said it was a very powerful object, and that its history was filled with death and betrayal."

Charlie listened for several moments. "This psychic is reliable, although last night I wasn't sure I believed her. But then someone tried to kill me. What she said was true; it is powerful. Maybe the item is even cursed. I'm not taking any more risks. From now on it's you and me, man to man. If you still want the item, you come get it yourself."

Juliana's heart was pounding. The part about the psychic was inspired.

"I understand you're a busy man. I was, too, until men came to kill me. Now I'm looking out for me."

Juliana breathed quietly as Charlie listened to Gutierrez. "I'll be in Ensenada for a few days. Maybe a priest at the mission can exorcise the curse from the item. Or maybe I can find a Mayan priestess to transfer the power to me. Money can buy almost anything in Mexico. You have my number if you decide to complete our business." He hung up.

Juliana's breath whooshed out. "He could send anybody in his place. We don't know what he looks like."

"He wants the power you saw in the sculpture. I could tell that priestess comment shook him. I think he'll come."

"And if he doesn't?"

"I have to hope that he does."

They stopped at the first rest stop they saw. There was one other car in the parking lot, and a man was exiting the building. As he drove away, Juliana followed Charlie into the women's rest room. They washed his arm and side, drying the wounds well. The bullet crease on his side looked red and painful.

Juliana sighed. "I wish I'd thought to bring the alcohol."

"Save your wishes for bigger things."

She bandaged him the best she could. She hoped her cousin knew a discreet medic.

"I think we need to tape the sculpture to my chest again." Charlie fingered it in his bag.

"I don't think that's a good idea. You're wounded."

"I can't risk the Mexican officials finding it if they search the car."

Juliana sighed her acquiescence and repeated the taping job they'd done at Montgomery's house. Then she helped Charlie into his oversized T-shirt and long-sleeved Chambray shirt with the sleeves rolled up. They found spare trash bags in a broom closet, wadded up his bloody shirt and towels and threw the bag away. Juliana used a wet paper towel to scrub at the blood on Charlie's jeans.

"Careful," he warned, smiling, "You're gonna make me horny caressing me like that."

"You're always horny."

"All the better for you, Jules."

"True. But I'd like to wait until we get to Ensenada, if you can control your hormones until then."

He gave her a put-upon face. "You're asking a lot."

"I'll make it worth your while."

His blue eyes heated. "I'll hold you to that."

Juliana ran a palm up his cock, which was swelling under his fly. He sucked in his breath. "That's a taste. I'll taste more when we have privacy."

"Tease." His voice was husky.

"I'm a sure thing where you're concerned, Charlie."

He licked his lips, pulled her close and kissed her long and hard.

When they returned to the car, Charlie pulled two guns with silencers from under the seat.

"Where'd you get those?" Juliana's voice rose.

"Our attackers." He unscrewed the silencers. "We need to hide these."

"You can't smuggle guns over the border!"

"Watch me. I'm tired of being an unarmed target."

"Those are dangerous!"

"I practice regularly at a firing range with a friend of mine. Just because I don't own a gun doesn't mean I don't know how to use one."

"Oh." She eyed them. As a cop's daughter she'd lived around guns her whole life. But Charlie and a gun? He was morphing again before her eyes.

Charlie gave her his sexy, lopsided smile. "I'm armed and dangerous, Jules."

Juliana snorted. "You're completely at my mercy when you see my pussy."

He choked back a laugh. "Who plunders whom? I'm the one with the nightstick."

"C'mon, stud. I think those weapons will fit in my makeup bag."

"I know where one weapon will fit."

"Too bad we don't have a thigh strap. I've always wanted to pack heat under my skirt."

"You do pack heat." His pupils dilated with remembrance. "God, are you hot down there."

Charlie caressed her back. Juliana felt his leashed need. He wanted her right here and now. She wanted to climb in the back seat with him and let him search her heat with his concealed weapon. But the sun was already up. They'd lost almost a half hour tending his wounds.

They tucked the guns in her luggage. It was a huge risk taking them through customs, but not the greatest risk they were taking on this venture. Gutierrez wasn't even the biggest threat. No, Charlie was the greatest peril … to her heart.

CHAPTER 20

Juliana's cousin, Felipe Sanchez, looked nothing like her, although the resemblance to her father was startling. Whereas Captain Sanchez was built like a heavyweight boxer, Felipe was more of a middleweight and a few years younger. His straight hair was blacker than the Captain's, and where Juliana's father had cold cop eyes, Felipe's warm gaze and easy smile welcomed the visitors to his home.

"Juliana's *novio*," Felipe greeted Charlie in Spanish, pumping his hand vigorously. "I know Dolores and Alejandro prayed for this day."

He released Charlie's hand, frowning. "Ziffkin. Where have I heard that name before?"

"Charlie grew up next door to me," Juliana explained.

Felipe pointed at Charlie. "*You* are the one. The one who tried to take Juliana's virtue when she was sixteen."

Geez, the story had made it all the way to Mexico. "Yeah, that's me."

"You waited a long time to claim her."

"I needed to prove myself first."

Felipe nodded. "Yes, that is the way with young men. Did you prove yourself?"

"I'm still working on it."

"That's why we're here, cousin," Juliana said. "Can we sit down and tell you what you've invited into your home?"

"You are always welcome here, cousin, no matter what the circumstances." Felipe led them through the airy whitewashed house into the dining room.

"Sit. Would you like something to drink? Rosita will be home in an hour to cook the noon meal."

"Something cold would be welcome," Charlie said.

When they were seated with tall cold bottles of Pepsi before them, Juliana told her cousin everything about the sculpture and Gutierrez.

When she finished, her cousin frowned fiercely. "But this is too dangerous for you, Juliana. You should turn it over to the police, to your father."

Juliana's face reddened. "My father can't help with this. The DEA told us they can't help either. We can't count on anyone in law enforcement. We're the only ones who can do this."

Felipe made horizontal slicing motions with his hands. "No, I forbid it. Your father would want me to."

"Juliana, would you help me untape the sculpture?" Charlie grimaced. "It's digging into my rib cage."

Juliana frowned but rose and came to his side. Charlie watched Felipe's face as he lifted his T-shirt. The older man looked shocked and then surprised.

"Hunahpu," Felipe breathed. "The Hero Twins. I recognize this likeness. I read of them at university. That looks old."

"It is." Juliana began to pull off the tape.

"Let me see if I remember," Felipe said. "He and his brother, Xbalanque, tricked and defeated the god of the Underworld. Why would a drug lord want something with a reputation like that?"

"Perhaps he's not thinking of his own defeat but of besting his competition, maybe outwitting the authorities," Juliana said. She pulled off the last strip of tape. Charlie rubbed the raw spot at the top of his chest.

Juliana handed Felipe the sculpture. "Do you want to know what I feel when I touch this?"

Felipe's brown eyes grew huge. He swallowed. "No. I can see in your face it disturbs you to touch it. I do not try to understand your gift or the burden it sometimes places on you."

He looked down at the sculpture, stroking it. "Powerful men covet old and valuable things. Who does this belong to?"

"I don't know," she said. "I haven't had time to think about that."

"Perhaps you should. If this person is alive, they can help you fight this Gutierrez." Felipe looked up. "I am not sure about your young man, and you are not a warrior, Juliana."

"Cousin, we don't have time to find the owner if they're alive. It might take days or weeks to get to wherever the sculpture came from. We only have now. Will you help us?"

Felipe shrugged. "What can *I* do? I manage a hotel."

"If Gutierrez comes to Mexico, we need eyes and ears. In the meantime, we need to hide. Charlie and I need to be relatives who've come for a visit."

Felipe smiled. "You are that."

"But I think Charlie needs to lose his last name. It's too distinctive. He can become Charles Sanchez, my husband."

Charlie nodded. "Yes, with my brown contacts and dark hair, I can pass for a Sanchez. Juliana's never been to Ensenada before, so no one here knows her."

Felipe sighed. "I will ask the Sanchezes who live closest. We have cousins, nieces, and nephews in Tecate, Rosarito, and Mexicali. Family helps family."

Charlie slumped as the tension drained from him. "We'll have to drop Hessler's name around town to get the word out." He rubbed the center of his forehead. "I can't think anymore."

"You're tired. It's been a long night," Juliana said. "Felipe, Charlie needs medical treatment, very discreet."

"I saw the bandages. Let me see what I can do."

"I think Charlie and I would like to take a shower before Rosita comes home."

Felipe rose, smiling. "I'll show you to your room."

It was an airy room with okra-colored walls and a wildly colorful bedspread in yellow, brown, and red. The colored pots in the window reminded Charlie of Juliana's apartment.

Charlie let Juliana lead him into the tiled bathroom. When he stripped off his clothes, his shirt clung to the tape residue. He needed her to scrub it off him. She peeled off her clothes, exposing the firm, shapely flesh he loved. So feminine, so inviting, so arousing. His cock came to attention.

She pulled him into the shower, and he gritted his teeth while she scrubbed him. Then her soapy hands slid way below the tape lines to boldly stroke his cock to spike-like firmness. She soaped his balls and between his buttocks. He bit back a groan as she teased his anus.

"The tape, Juliana." If she didn't finish that job, he was going to be finished.

Juliana scrubbed his back, and when she turned him, his hands were full of soap. He spread it over her breasts. Her nipples were aroused to points that stabbed his palms. He massaged them thoroughly before sliding his hand down her slightly rounded abdomen to her mound. He slipped his hands between her legs, running his slippery fingers from her clit to her anus. Juliana moaned. He circled her opening with one hand while stroking her clit with the other. She leaned hard against him.

Removing his hands, he slid his cock between her legs. As he lifted her enough to slide inside her, she clung to him.

"Charlie, give it all to me."

He did, several times, then: "You said something about tasting."

He turned off the water. Juliana slid down his body to her knees. She licked from the tip of his cock to the base. It felt like heaven. She placed her mouth on the head and slowly took him inside the tight warmth. He groaned.

She released him slowly, sucking hard, and then swallowed him again. He shuddered with pleasure. Again she released him, sucking the loose skin before taking his length inside once more. He tensed on the edge of orgasm. Once more, and he'd come. But he didn't want to come that way.

Charlie pulled loose, pushed her to her back, and followed her down. He nestled between her thighs and thrust inside. The pleasure was intense. He shifted on her, sliding deeper. She raised her hips and deepened his penetration. In three thrusts he came, driving hard into her.

Charlie raised his head and kissed her. "How was that, Mrs. Sanchez?"

"Wonderful, Mr. Sanchez. Did I redeem my promise?"

"For now. I'll need to be serviced again soon. I have a high-performance engine, you know."

"Your piston works just fine."

"A well-lubricated cylinder helps it slide home."

"Oh, is that what you were doing?"

"You bet. Did you really need a nap?" he asked.

"If you have the energy, there's a spot between my legs that needs a little more attention."

"Oh?"

"I promise it won't take long."

"You're that ready?"

"I'm afraid so."

Charlie rolled her over onto her knees and lifted her bottom. He spread her and placed his mouth over her pussy, sucking. She rewarded him with groans. He laved the tender flesh, probing inside her. Then he sucked her clit. She shifted and groaned. He ran his tongue down to her pussy and probed and sucked some more. Little rhythmic strains and groans escaped her lips, and she shuddered all over with her orgasm. It turned him on. Damn, but she made him horny with his face in her pussy. He pulled out his hot rod to take her for another ride.

CHAPTER 21

For two days Charlie and Juliana had done Ensenada and each other. They'd danced in the discothèque and between the sheets. They'd walked from one end of town to the other under the watchful eyes of Mexican cops patrolling with machine guns; they watched a cruise ship dock, cruised the peer, made love in the ocean, visited shrines, missions, museums, and her relatives.

Eleven Sanchez cousins arrived from the surrounding towns. Charlie and Juliana spent much of their time with the ones in their twenties, including Ricarda, Alfonso, Estebon, Jose, and Lorenzo. The huge Sanchez clan accepted Charlie as Juliana's fiancé. Rosita blatantly encouraged them to seek the priest to make it legal.

Gutierrez remained frustratingly silent. Charlie had been certain he'd come.

Although cousins surrounded them wherever they went, Charlie didn't feel safe. It wasn't just because the Mexican cops randomly stopped cars to check papers, putting their cover constantly in jeopardy. Gutierrez was wily. He lived his life off the radar. Charlie wouldn't put it past the drug lord to arrive in Ensenada unannounced. It was a sure bet no one would check *his* papers.

Felipe and Rosita had told them there was a dark side to glittering Ensenada. Parties seemed to go on nonstop, with the California crowd letting loose south of the border. And drugs played a part in some of that activity. Mexican officials outwardly denounced it, but with money changing hands, they looked the other way.

Ensenada was Gutierrez's natural habitat; Gutierrez's people.

Charlie wasn't the only one who felt uneasy. Juliana's stiff posture and the tight lines around her eyes revealed her tension. Charlie rubbed her arm. "Relax."

"I feel like I'm being watched."

"That's your cousins. Or the cops."

"No. It's more."

He tensed. "You can't sense him."

"No. I wish we had a photo of him so I could find him. I think he's here."

Charlie wrapped an arm around her. "If he is, he doesn't know who we are or what we look like either. Our car is covered under a tarp, so no one knows it's American. We're Mr. and Mrs. Sanchez. Not Jordan Hessler and his lover."

Juliana rubbed at the goose bumps on her arms. "Don't say things like that."

"He'll call," Charlie assured her.

"He's cautious. He'll look before he leaps. And he won't be alone."

"We're not alone either."

"They're trained to kill. We're not."

"I'll take him with me if he tries." Charlie carried a gun he'd use if he had to. Another reason not to let the cops stop him. But he needed to lighten Juliana's mood. "Let's go shopping. Rosita's birthday is next week."

"All right." She gave him a bright smile.

Hessler's phone rang and nearly stopped Charlie's heart. And then it galloped madly. Juliana clutched his arm. He took a deep breath, looked at the number and opened the phone. "Hessler." Juliana pressed her ear close.

"You're a hard man to find," Gutierrez's smooth Spanish voice said. "You're everywhere but you're nowhere."

"I told you I'm in Ensenada."

"I'm here. I've come to collect what you owe me."

"Where and when?"

"Tonight. Midnight. Pier 80, slip 42, the Sandpiper."

"I'll be there." Charlie closed the phone.

"How do we know it's not a trap?" Juliana demanded.

"We don't. So we get there first."

They caught a taxi to Pier 80 with Ricarda and Alfonso Sanchez. Charlie scanned the area. This didn't feel right. "We're a group of young people out to see a friend off. Look for slip 42, but don't indicate you've seen it. Then look for someone casting off. We'll watch them leave then come back here. Everyone got the plan?"

Ricarda and Alfonso agreed. They were from two different branches of the Sanchez family. Ricarda was twenty and stringbean thin with straight black hair down to her hips. Alfonso was the same age but muscular with a sharp mustache.

The women paired up and strolled casually past slip 42. Charlie saw nothing unusual about the large sailboat. It looked like it was locked up tight, the sail lashed down. He continued walking to where the women had stopped ten slips further down. A group of people were making preparations to depart.

Juliana and Ricarda made small talk with the boat's occupants. Charlie's neck itched as the time crawled by. Were these boaters amateurs? How long did it take to launch a boat? At length they cast off, and his group waved the travelers goodbye.

Then he escorted Juliana off the pier with her cousins following.

"I didn't see anyone at slip 42," Alfonso said.

"No activity at all," Charlie agreed. "Keep walking."

They strolled along five more piers before they hailed a cab.

"What does it mean?" Ricarda asked. "If he called from there, someone should be there."

"True," Charlie said.

"If he was watching the pier," Juliana mused, "he can guess Hessler is either you or Alfonso."

"Or that I'm not Hessler," Charlie replied.

Juliana and her cousins looked confused, so Charlie explained. "If he knows what Hessler looks like, and if we're the only ones who went down that pier, then he knows I'm not Hessler."

Juliana gripped his arm. Her eyes were wide. "What are we going to do?"

"We'll set up around that slip. Then at midnight, I'll arrive with the sculpture, and we'll capture him." Charlie knew it was simplistic. Mexican officials probably wouldn't prosecute Gutierrez. U.S. law enforcement was also constrained. But he couldn't stop now. He had to go forward.

He instructed the taxi driver to take them to the market. They wandered around for an hour before he felt sure they hadn't been followed. Then he guided his little group home.

Fifteen people sat around the table for dinner. An expectant hush fell while they ate. They wanted this to be finished. Charlie glanced at Juliana's beloved face. He didn't want their time together to be over. Maybe after they caught Gutierrez... Would he have proven himself worthy of happiness then? He *had* to because being with her again had showed him how empty and lonely his life was. Glamorous California paled beside the vibrant colors with which Juliana filled her life. And the excitement of being surrounded by Hollywood stars and glittering events failed to move him like the shining love in Juliana's eyes when she looked at him. The same way she'd looked at him for years and he'd taken it for granted. Never again.

At nine-thirty, four of the young Sanchezes left for the pier. They took Charlie's baseball bat, assorted iron bars, pipes, and lengths of wood with them. The clock ticked the minutes away. The tension in the house was thick and uncomfortable. Felipe played quiet Spanish music on his guitar. It made the waiting a little more bearable.

Hessler's phone rang, and Charlie nearly jumped out of his skin. He wasn't the only one. Felipe hit a jarring note.

Charlie looked at the phone, saw Gutierrez's number and opened it. "Hessler."

"We both know you are not him." Gutierrez sounded smug.

Charlie covered the mouthpiece. "He knows."

"What is your game?" Gutierrez asked.

"Power. The same as yours."

"It is funny you should say that. I have someone here who wants to speak to you...Mr. Sanchez."

"Charlie, don't do what he says!" Alfonso yelled on the other end of the line, his voice trumpeting into the room.

Felipe and Rosita looked stricken.

"You think *children* can outsmart me?" Gutierrez sneered. "You have one hour to produce the Hunahpu before I kill them. You understand?"

Charlie's stomach tied in knots. "Yes."

"Same place. Come alone. Bring the Hunahpu. Leave it and walk away."

"Yeah, and you're such a nice guy you'll let them go."

"You do not have the power in this negotiation. I do." A scream of pain nearly shattered Charlie's eardrum.

Rosita and Felipe clutched one another. The rest of the Sanchezes paled.

Gutierrez continued in a conversational tone, "The little girl just lost a finger. If you do not bring the sculpture, she loses her life and the others, too."

"Bastard!" Charlie snarled.

"You are out of my league. Do what you are told, and your young friends live." Gutierrez severed the connection.

"Gutierrez has them." Anger and fear washed over Charlie in hot and cold waves. God, his fault again.

The Sanchezes gasped, cried, and moaned. Juliana clutched his arm.

"He says he's going to kill them if I don't bring the sculpture to him in an hour."

"Holy Mother of God! Give it to him!" Rosita cried.

"He'll kill them anyway," Charlie said.

"If there is a chance … " she cried.

"There isn't. He's evil. He glories in other people's suffering." He had to stop Gutierrez.

Rosita sobbed, and Felipe tucked her against his chest. He turned to Charlie. "Who screamed?"

"Ricarda. He … hurt her."

Rosita cried out as though she'd suffered the hurt herself.

Felipe's eyes hardened, making him look more like Captain Sanchez than ever. "Then he must not get away with it. No one hurts a Sanchez without repercussions."

"I can find Ricarda and the others," Juliana said into the tense silence. "Their clothes are here."

"Then do it," Rosita cried. "I cannot tell their mothers they died."

"We'll be going where an unknown number of men are armed and on the alert," Juliana warned. "It will be very dangerous."

"Just get me close enough," Charlie said, "and I'll take it from there. None of you need risk yourselves further." He'd get the young people out or die trying.

"We're going with you," one cousin said.

Another nodded in agreement. "You need us."

Charlie shook his head.

"I'm coming, too." Felipe's look dared Charlie to argue. "You don't have to prove yourself alone."

"No!" Rosita clutched him.

"I have to go, *amore*. They are my blood."

Charlie swore he'd bring everyone back alive. He'd been an extra in enough war movies and watched enough hours of film to have at least Hollywood's version of going up against bad guys. "I have two guns. Anyone else have one and know how to use it? I don't want to get shot by friendly fire."

Felipe stood. "I have guns in the cellar."

"I have a knife and can use that," one cousin said.

Charlie rose. "Let's go."

Juliana gathered cast-off clothing from the four cousins. Charlie armed himself, and had her tape the sculpture to his chest once more. Felipe and the others climbed the stairs from the cellar, tucking guns into waistbands and pockets.

At Charlie's raised eyebrows, Felipe said simply, "I have not always managed a hotel."

The cousin's knife turned out to be a wickedly sharp Bowie knife, ten inches long.

Where had these Sanchezes gotten weapons like this and why? What had Felipe done or been in the past? Charlie didn't ask for details. This wasn't the United States; the government here was different.

They piled into two cabs. Charlie sat beside Juliana in the first car. White-faced, she clutched the clothes and called out directions to the driver. The cab turned onto the waterfront and headed for some warehouses, where she told the driver to stop.

They exited, and the taxis drove away. Charlie could just see Pier 80 from where he stood. Everyone huddled in the shadows.

"This warehouse?" Charlie asked, keeping his voice low.

"No. The last one we passed. I didn't want to stop there."

"Do you know where they are inside?"

"Toward the back. I need to get closer."

Charlie didn't want her any closer, but he needed the hostages' exact location. "C'mon."

Their group crept to the warehouse two abreast, making no sound. Juliana led them into the alley between the two buildings. When they were two-thirds of the way to the end of the structure, she halted.

"Here." Her voice was a wisp of sound.

"How close to this wall?" Charlie asked.

She cocked her head. He could barely see her in the crescent moonlight. "Ten feet?"

"Not close enough." He led the group around the back of the building, past a door, and rounded the next corner.

"They're closer on the other side," Juliana whispered.

Charlie stationed Felipe and two cousins at the back entrance. He and Juliana and the rest trouped back to where she'd sensed the captives were closest. There were windows in the wall. Two young cousins boosted a third up.

"I see them," the slender young man hissed with excitement. He tried the window, then signaled to be let down.

"The window is locked," the cousin reported. "We could break it, but that would make noise. They're sitting in a circle with their hands and feet tied." Anger laced his young voice. "One man is guarding them with a gun."

"He didn't see you, did he?" Any second Charlie feared an armed attack.

"No, he was facing away from the window. But Alfonso did."

"I pray to God he doesn't give us away," one cousin said with fervor.

"Let's go talk to Felipe," Charlie said.

The cousin reported what he'd seen.

Felipe said, "There are two doors in the front, one of which is a truck door, one in the back, and windows on the side. This door is locked."

"The front may be locked too." Charlie looked at his watch. "We're running out of time."

"There's a forklift parked in the field behind us," the cousin named Estebon said. "If I can get it started, I can operate it."

"A frontal assault?" Charlie asked. "Ram the front gates?"

"Excellent idea," Felipe said. "I can shoot the guard through the window." What was it like to live in a seemingly modern, civilized city and yet know how to defend yourself and the ones you loved like he planned to do?

"We shoot through the windows as we ram the front door. Two people remain at the back door to prevent anyone from escaping," Charlie summarized.

The Sanchezes nodded.

"I'll go with Estebon and the forklift," Charlie said. Juliana looked at him with wide, fearful eyes.

"I'm going in the front," another cousin, Jose, volunteered.

"Me, too," offered Lorenzo.

"Estebon, try the forklift," Charlie ordered.

Time passed. Muffled night sounds floated from the direction of the pier. Louder and closer was someone's sneaker scuffing a stone. Salt brine tickled Charlie's nose, along with food smells and sewer gas.

When the engine fired, its growl split the night. Most of their little raiding party jumped. Charlie's heart thudded in his chest. Estebon raised a fist in triumph, then he put the forklift in gear and headed toward the side alley. The two cousins guarding the back door pulled out their guns and took their position.

The engine echoed loudly in the confined alley. Charlie held his gun ready for trouble. He made sure Juliana was behind him.

They left Felipe, three cousins, and Juliana at the window. Charlie gave her a quick kiss. She gripped his hand hard. Then he, Jose, and Lorenzo ran after the forklift. It moved faster than he'd thought a machine like that could. Before he was ready, the forklift turned the corner around the front.

Under the single weak overhead light, Estebon turned the forklift to face the warehouse. The truck door was a wooden one that rolled up.

Estebon gunned the engine and raced for the door. The forks crashed through the wood with satisfying ease, destroying the majority of the door with a crack that resounded over the water. Charlie followed the forklift through the hole and dived for cover behind a stack of wooden pallets. Jose followed him and tucked in behind Charlie's back. When the forklift engine shut off, the silence was deafening. There was a pop, and something thudded into the wood to his left. Gutierrez's men were shooting at them. With his gun ready, Charlie peered into the dimness but saw no one except Estebon crouching behind the two-high stack of crates across from him.

Lorenzo somersaulted through the smashed door. In front of the forklift, one of Gutierrez's men rose from his hiding position. Charlie fired at him. With a cry of pain the man fell back. Lorenzo slid in beside Estebon.

"We need to get behind them," Charlie whispered to Jose. The young man nodded. Charlie signaled to Lorenzo and Estebon.

They darted forward to a stack of shipping crates. A gunshot sounded, and wood splintered above their heads. Lorenzo returned fire with two quick shots.

Charlie and Jose scrambled for the next crates in the row. Charlie signaled Lorenzo forward, then took aim so Lorenzo could move.

From the back of the warehouse, gunshots boomed. It didn't sound like there was return fire. Charlie prayed Felipe's group had gotten the hostages out of the way. At least Juliana was outside in relative safety.

Charlie's trio leapfrogged deeper into the warehouse. He heard a cry of pain from the hostages' location, and his chest tightened. Please, God, not a Sanchez!

A shape appeared from behind a stack of crates to his left. Charlie couldn't turn in time! Suddenly Jose pointed his gun over Charlie's shoulder and fired. The man fell backward out of sight.

"Thanks," Charlie breathed.

"No problem, cousin." Jose's smile flashed white in the darkness.

They scrambled forward to find a man clutching his chest. Even as they watched, his arms and hands relaxed and his eyes closed.

Silence echoed in the warehouse. Charlie waited with his gun ready. Across the open space, Lorenzo raised his hands in a questioning gesture. Cautiously, the four of them rose. Charlie saw no movement. He pressed forward, the three cousins beside him. They met no resistance, so they kept moving. A dark head appeared around a stack of crates. Their guns aimed toward it, but a hand waved at them, and Alfonso appeared from the dimness.

"Are we secured?" he whispered.

"Don't know yet," Charlie replied.

Felipe appeared behind Alfonso with a group of dark-haired cousins, including the hostages. "We got two of their guys."

"We did, too," Charlie said. He jittered. He didn't like being here. "Got everybody?"

"Yes. We came in through the back door, so no one's left guarding it." Felipe's gaze darted around the warehouse. "Let's get out of here."

They turned toward the front.

"Sanchez!" Gutierrez's voice boomed. "I want the Hunahpu." A man appeared in the wrecked warehouse doorway under the light. He had an arm wrapped around Juliana's throat, with a gun pointed at her head.

Shit, not Juliana! Not the woman Charlie loved.

CHAPTER 22

Juliana strained at Gutierrez's hold around her neck. She'd been so stupid to openly peer into the warehouse because she was worried about Charlie. Now Gutierrez would hurt both of them, because of her. She'd just regained the love and light of her life, and Gutierrez intended to take that away.

No! This time she'd defy fate. She wanted more time with Charlie. She struggled against Gutierrez.

Felipe and her cousins aimed their guns at Gutierrez, at her. Their faces looked strained.

Charlie aimed at Gutierrez's forehead. "Let her go."

"A bunch of amateurs cannot defeat me. I'll kill her." He jammed the gun painfully into the side of her head.

She needed Charlie to know how she felt, before it was too late. "I love you, Charlie."

Charlie's eyes gleamed. He advanced on them, still aiming at Gutierrez. "You harm her, and you're dead. I have no compunction about killing you."

"You are weak. All of you. And I am strong. I hold a power base you cannot even dream of."

"I hold the Hunahpu with hundreds of years of power," Charlie said. "A power that belongs to me now."

"No!" Gutierrez snarled. "It is mine." His gun swung toward Charlie.

No! She wouldn't let him hurt Charlie. Juliana threw all her weight against Gutierrez's arm. The gun discharged, the boom deafening in her ear. She tore herself out of Gutierrez's grip, her momentum turning her 360 degrees. There were a dozen return shots from her cousins, the noise thunderous in the warehouse.

Charlie clutched his chest and fell backward.

"Charlie!" Juliana screamed. *God, no!* She lurched toward him.

Felipe and her cousins ran toward her through the haze of gun smoke, but she had eyes only for one man. She fell to her knees by Charlie. There was a small round hole in his T-shirt.

"Charlie, please don't die! I love you. Please!" She tore at his shirt. Her cousins knelt around Charlie, their faces creased with worry. She heard Felipe moving behind her, by Gutierrez.

There was no blood. Her desperate fingers searched around the sculpture's edges. Where had the bullet entered?

"The sculpture stopped the bullet," Alfonso said, sounding awed. His hand snaked past Juliana's to touch the sculpture, now clearly cracked.

Metal reflected the light. Juliana's shaking hands touched the hot bit where it lodged in the sculpture. Her seeking hands found unbroken skin underneath. "Thank God."

Charlie groaned. "What hit me, the forklift?" He rubbed his chest and slowly sat up. "This damn thing."

"That *damn thing* saved your life." Her voice quavered.

The cousins laughed nervously.

"It stopped the bullet," Alfonso said.

Juliana and her cousins pulled Charlie to his feet. He staggered to Gutierrez's body. "Is he dead?"

"Yes," Felipe confirmed with savage satisfaction, rising from the body.

"Bastard," Ricarda spat. The hand she gripped to her chest had a strip of colored cloth torn from the bottom of her shirt wrapped around it.

"Who killed him?" Charlie asked.

"Does it matter?" Felipe asked. "He's dead."

"I don't want any of you to get in trouble."

"And you want it to be you," Juliana guessed.

Charlie nodded, his face expressionless. "Yeah."

"The Hunahpu killed him. That and his greed for it. Give me the sculpture." Felipe held out his hands.

Charlie ripped the two chunks from the tape and handed them over.

Felipe held them overhead and hurled them to the cement floor where they smashed into pieces. His smile was viciously satisfied. "No one else will have to die for this thing. We'd better move. Someone had to have reported gunfire by now."

Charlie stared at the debris and nodded. "*Gracias*, Felipe. Let's go home."

Alfonso hissed from near the ruined door, "Police! Many of them."

"Not again," Charlie muttered.

Juliana fought panic, but Felipe ordered in a harsh voice, "Out the back. Quickly, and be quiet about it."

He led the way to the back door, around a body, and out into air not tainted by gun smoke. They darted into the grass where the forklift had been parked, and found a graveyard of old Volkswagen cars. The cousins spread out, running as fast as they could around the carcasses. Juliana held on tight to Charlie's hand.

They couldn't be arrested. Mexican authorities didn't like Americans, and in Mexico you were guilty until proven innocent. She, Charlie, and her cousins might be held for months or years until they could prove their innocence … or pay a hefty ransom. If the cops didn't sell them to the drug lords first. She ran faster.

Felipe signaled to the left and they exited the field onto a narrow street. He kept them moving at a fast walk until they approached a seedy-looking bar. He stopped them under the weak light and glanced around the group. Juliana did, too. She spotted a bloody arm, Lorenzo had a bleeding cheek, and Estebon was holding up another cousin, who had blood on his trousers. They looked like what they were: survivors of a war.

Felipe helped clean up the obvious blood and made sure the guns were tucked out of sight. Alfonso tied a bandana around his cousin's bleeding arm. Ricarda ripped another strip from her shirt and tied it around her cousin's leg, under his pants.

"Those of you who are injured, stay in the center. We'll catch a taxi in a few blocks and then switch taxis at the market. We'll be home soon."

Charlie coached them. "We're just a group of young people out for the evening."

"But cousin Felipe is not young," Alfonso objected.

Ricarda moved to Felipe's side and slid her uninjured arm around him. "He is my *novio*." Her tone dared Alfonso to say anything further.

Felipe curled his arm around her shoulders. "Let's go."

Charlie slid his arm around Juliana, and she welcomed his warmth. They were alive, and he knew she loved him. Now they needed to get to safety.

When they exited the narrow street onto a wider one, a police car headed toward them. Felipe, Ricarda, Charlie, and Juliana moved to the front of the group and waited for the police car to crawl by. The cops were looking over everyone on the street. It stopped in front of their group and the cop shined a flashlight at them. Juliana feared her heart would beat out of her chest. She hoped he didn't pay attention to her and Ricarda's shirts and shoes. Mexican women wore pretty high-heeled shoes and feminine blouses that showed cleavage, while the two of them wore flats, and T-shirts suited to skulking.

"What are all of you doing?" the cop growled. He wore a fierce scowl.

"My *novio's* cousins are visiting from Tecate," Felipe answered. "They wanted to try a bar they'd heard about, but it's not a very nice place."

The cop looked down the narrow street behind them. "No it isn't. Take your cousins to a better part of town. You're old enough to know better."

"Yes, sir."

The car rolled forward down the street. Juliana breathed a sigh of relief.

"Let's go." Felipe directed them through a warren of streets until they came out on the other side of the harbor. There they flagged down taxis and heard about the excitement on the docks.

Nearly three hours later, after the same discreet medic who had treated Charlie's wounds treated the wounded cousins, they sat around Felipe's dining room table and shared the story with Rosita. She clucked and fussed over them, bringing out food and tequila, and hugging them all.

All the while, Juliana wanted to be alone with Charlie so they could discuss her declaration of love and how he felt about it.

"I guess you'll return home now that your task is done," Alfonso said. "Will we be invited to the wedding?"

"Of course," Rosita said. "What date have you chosen?"

Juliana hedged. "We just got engaged. We've been too preoccupied the past few days to plan anything. I don't know how much we can afford."

"Nonsense," Rosita said. "Have the wedding in Mexico, and it will cost less."

Juliana gave Charlie a helpless look.

"Rosita, they are Americans," Felipe chided gently. "They may want to marry in their own country."

She planted her hands on her hips. "I don't know how big his family is, but it can't be larger than ours."

Charlie's smile blazed. "I have a small family."

"See." Rosita waved a hand at Charlie. "Small."

"If you decide to marry here, you could use the hotel I manage," Felipe offered. "You've seen the missions. You could have the ceremony there. Our church is beautiful, too. And we could smooth everything with the priest."

"I'm not Catholic," Charlie said.

Everyone stared at him.

"Not Catholic," Rosita repeated, as though he'd said he was from another planet. Then she lifted her chin. "You'll convert, of course."

Charlie sputtered a laugh. "Of course."

Juliana gaped at him. Was he truly committing to this?

Charlie looked at her, and she felt herself falling into the heated warmth of his eyes. She wished the brown contacts gone. "I love Juliana. I'd do anything for her."

"Are you sure?" The words were a wisp of sound, all she could squeeze out of her tight throat.

"I've never been more certain in my life."

Juliana threw herself into his arms, nearly knocking him out of his chair. "I love you, Charlie." She'd be with him forever.

"I love you, too."

As he kissed her, Rosita said, "See, it will be a good Catholic wedding. I'll call Dolores tomorrow and we'll arrange everything."

•••

Distant pounding jerked Charlie awake the next morning. Through bleary eyes, he saw it was seven-fifteen. His heart raced. Who'd be at the door at this hour?

Juliana lifted her head from his arm. "Trouble?" That one word was laced with fear.

"It can't be the police, can it?" But even as he asked the question, he slipped from the bed. He stepped into his jeans and grabbed the gun from the dresser.

"Don't go out there armed!" Juliana threw on his T-shirt and tugged on her panties.

As they exited their bedroom, they met Felipe and Rosita in the hall.

"Don't worry," Felipe said. "We didn't leave a trail. The police can't trace us here." But lines furrowed his forehead. He wore only his trousers … and his gun tucked into the back of them.

In the living room, the younger cousins turned wide, anxious, bleary eyes to them from their sleeping bags. Most of them were armed, Charlie noted.

The pounding came again. As Felipe walked to the door, most of the cousins stood up. Charlie stayed back a little ways, gripping Juliana's hand. He'd fight if he had to, but he hoped it didn't come to that.

Felipe opened the door.

Juliana's father stood there, with Rick Ziffkin behind him. "Felipe, I'm sorry to arrive unannounced, but—"

"Papá!" Juliana cried, her face a mix of relief and horror.

"Uncle Alejandro!" Estebon cried.

"Felipe," her father glowered at the group of them, including Charlie.

"Hello, Alejandro," Felipe replied, smiling. "Come in."

Captain Sanchez crossed the threshold. Rick followed, his eyes locking on Charlie's.

"Charlie," he said, then couldn't seem to say more.

Charlie strode to his brother and was enveloped in a bear hug.

"We thought you were dead." Pain laced Rick's voice. He held Charlie at arm's length. "Agent Fuentes called to tell me he feared the worst, what with Hessler murdered and your apartment a bloody mess. You took years off my life, and Mom and Dad's, too. Despite what you may think, we love you. You should have called." Rick wrapped Charlie in a tight bear hug.

Charlie blinked back tears. "Sorry. We needed secrecy."

"I figured that out. Gutierrez's death made international news last night. Fuentes called and woke me when the story broke. We figured you might have had something to do with it."

"We did. All of us." Charlie indicated everyone in the room. Then he squinted, thinking. "It's only been a few hours. How did you get here so fast?"

"Captain Sanchez and I flew to Los Angeles to help look for the two of you. So we only had to drive down."

"Who is he?" Alfonso asked in Spanish, pointing at Rick.

"This is my brother, Rick," Charlie said.

"The small family," Rosita crowed with delight. "Come into the dining room, and I'll make breakfast."

"But cousin," Jose complained, "we've only been asleep a few hours."

"Get your lazy self to the table," she ordered. "Can't you see Alejandro and Charlie's brother want to hear the tale? They are tired and hungry. Where are your manners?" She chased everyone to the dining room.

Charlie managed to extricate Juliana from her father's arms and sit beside her.

For the second time in four hours, they relayed the tale, only this time Charlie and Juliana started from the attack on them in his apartment. Poor Rick understood only a smattering of Spanish, so one of the bilingual cousins translated for him.

"So you see why we needed secrecy," Charlie said. "We needed Montgomery's men fixed on L.A."

"They caught Montgomery's man staking out your apartment," Captain Sanchez told him. "The California police tied him to Montgomery, so Montgomery's under investigation for murder for hire."

"What about the man in my apartment?" Charlie asked.

"There was no other man," Rick reported, frowning.

Charlie looked at Juliana.

Rick sighed. "I'll call Fuentes and tell him to look for a body. Was the blood in your apartment his?" He catalogued the bandages on Charlie's body and the huge dark bruise on his chest.

"Some of it."

Rick stared at him a long time, his expression inscrutable. "You didn't look surprised when I said Hessler had been murdered."

"We knew," Charlie replied. "We saw him."

Rick glared. "And you didn't report it."

"We needed to run. We'd already been shot at once that night. We weren't going to stand around and let somebody else use us for target practice."

"I don't know you at all anymore, do I?" his brother asked.

"No. I told you I'd changed. But you can learn who I am now."

"Yeah, I can."

"Alejandro, you can settle an argument now that you're here," Rosita began. "We were discussing whether to hold the wedding here or in America."

"Wedding?" Juliana's father asked, frowning.

Juliana held up her hand and Charlie's. "Surprise, Papá."

"Those are wedding rings." Captain Sanchez looked shocked, and then resigned. He ran a hand slowly down his face.

The younger cousins whooped with laughter. "They've been pretending to be married," Alfonso explained. "Mr. and Mrs. Sanchez. But really they're engaged."

Charlie squeezed Juliana's hand. Captain Sanchez didn't seem too averse to having him as a son-in-law. "We could probably get a priest Rosita knows to say the vows over us today if you want."

Rosita snorted.

Juliana poked him. "I want a big wedding. I want the whole world to know we were meant to be together."

Her father sighed. "The priest can marry you today. Later we'll have a big summer wedding. In America. We'll invite everyone. I'll pay."

Rosita clapped with glee.

"And you," Captain Sanchez pointed to Charlie. "I'll sponsor you into the Police Academy."

Rick looked stunned.

Charlie gaped. He thought of the Police Academy, and it sounded like the Army to him. Rules, regulations, schedules. He shuddered. "Thank you, Captain Sanchez, but no thanks. I'm a very *un*regulation guy. I don't do well with authority."

"How will you support my daughter and your children?" Captain Sanchez demanded.

"Papá, how old fashioned," Juliana protested.

"I make a small living as a private investigator. My business is very young. Although I'd been counting on Jordan Hessler's referrals to grow it. I can kiss that goodbye."

The captain looked thoughtful. "I have an old friend, an ex-cop, who's now a private eye. He gets a lot of business from Miami P.D., more than he can handle. I think he'd take you on as a partner."

Move back to Miami? Charlie looked at Juliana. Her Sanchez relatives in Mexico were only three hours away, right across the border. Her Miami family was five and a half hours away by plane. Did he have the right to take her away from her family?

He glanced at Rick. Being with the Sanchez clan had made Charlie recall how good it used to be with his brothers. If Rick, his parents, and his older brother, Michael, were ever to get to know the new Charlie and accept him as the Sanchezes had, he had to see them regularly. There was nothing for him in California anymore. He inhaled a large breath. Yes, it was time to go home.

"I'd appreciate if you'd talk to him for me," Charlie said.

"Tell him I'd like to work for him, too," Juliana added.

Captain Sanchez looked like he wanted to protest, but he swallowed whatever he'd planned to say. "Fine."

Rosita launched into plans to get them to the priest. The table broke up into excited chatter. Charlie used the commotion to take Juliana into his arms and kiss her breathless.

When they came up for air, Rosita was passing out glasses of tequila.

Felipe stood and raised his glass. "To the real Maya Hero Twins, Charlie and Juliana, who defeated their enemy through trickery."

"*Salute*," the cousins endorsed the toast.

Charlie kissed Juliana again. He'd triumphed over a lot more than Gutierrez to claim his soul mate, the other half of himself. They'd make every moment together count from now on. He thanked that damn sculpture for bringing them together once more.

About the Author

Multi-published author Shay Lacy lives in northwest Ohio with her photographer/graphic designer husband. She loves following the man of her dreams with a camera in hand and a pen and notebook in her backpack. Sensible secretary by day, romance author by night, when not lost in her imagination or reading a good book, she is likely researching her next book with a SWAT team ride-along or a visit to a DNA lab.

For more information about Shay or to see the books she's written, please visit her website at *www.shaylacy.com*.

More from This Author
(From *Counterpoint* by Shay Lacy)

Who sent this? Bryce Gannon wondered, as he turned over the thick brown padded envelope marked CONFIDENTIAL looking for the return address. But the criminal defense attorney found no clue. Did it contain something for a case? He worked at the tight seal with his letter opener, but just as his curiosity was about to be appeased his phone rang. With one hand he reached for it, his gaze shifting away from the envelope.

Boom. The envelope exploded, shooting white powder into the air, just missing Bryce's face. He jerked, dropping the envelope, which poofed another small cloud of white. What the hell ... ? He inhaled and choked on the dust.

A letter bomb.

From the outer office he heard a woman's frightened scream. His desk phone continued to shrill for his attention.

God, a bomb. He coughed, trying to wave away the white mist, until his brain finally kicked in. *Get up, you fool. Get away from this crap.*

Ramming his chair back from his desk, he sprang clear of the cloud. But he continued to cough. His right hand was covered with white and tingled from the explosion's percussion. The powder, whatever it was, blended into his stark white shirt.

"Bryce!" his office manager Sharron Rudgate shrieked from the doorway, "Are you hurt?" Her eyes were wild.

"Call nine-one-one," he managed, although it took all his breath to get those four syllables out. He couldn't seem to draw enough air into his lungs.

Sharron shouted his message into the hall before stepping towards him, her hand outstretched. He waved her back. He didn't want anyone else inhaling this crap. A young researcher appeared behind Sharron, her face white as she stared at him.

There was an awful taste in his mouth, more bitter than chemical. He couldn't seem to clear his throat. God, was it poison?

"Bryce, how much of that did you breathe in?" The usually unruffled Sharron sounded nearly hysterical. "What is it?"

Bryce couldn't answer either question. He couldn't breathe. His lungs screamed for air. His bronchial tubes spasmed painfully. His breath whistled as he drew it in. He tore at his silk tie, undoing the knot, and yanked at the button of his linen shirt collar so hard the button snapped off. But it didn't help. He clutched his throat with one hand and his chest with the other. His lungs were on fire.

His knees buckled, dumping him to the plush carpet.

Jesus, he was going to die.

"Bryce!" Sharron screamed. "Bryce, oh my God!"

Bryce had no breath to speak. There were more frightened faces in the doorway standing at a safe distance listening to the sound of his tortured breathing. His staff, his office, his legal practice. The trappings of his success.

He saw his life pass before his eyes and felt deeply disappointed. He'd never been in love, never married, and never had children. He'd gotten criminals off on technicalities to roam free to hurt more people. He'd accepted large amounts of money from them, like the check with lots of zeroes on it he got today from accused racketeer Adam Steele. It was dirty money, guilty money — *blood* money. Thirty pieces of silver to betray himself and the law he loved. He'd had so much promise coming out of law school … and *this* was what his life amounted to. He knelt on the thick carpet like a supplicant, pleading for his miserable life.

He didn't think he'd be cashing that check.

Suffocating hurt. He'd scream at the pain if he could, but he couldn't. His heart pounded in his ears, laboring hard. Black spots danced before his eyes. His friends needed him. It was too bad

Bryce would fail them at the end. He couldn't even pass on any messages to them. Dammit, he wanted to live. As his strength faded he sank to the carpet.

The world spun away with his regrets.

In the mood for more Crimson Romance?
Check out *Love Is in the Air* by
Anji Nolan at *CrimsonRomance.com*.